Five Days In May

Gary S Smith

Copyright © Gary S Smith 2012

The rights of Gary S Smith to be identified as the author of this book have been asserted, in accordance with the Copyright, Designs and Patent Act 1988

All rights reserved. No part of this publication may be reproduced, stored in any retrieval system, or transmitted in any form or by any means without the prior written permission of the publisher, nor be circulated by any form of binding or cover or than that which it is published and without a similar condition being imposed on the subsequent publisher.

ISBN: 9798679975910

First paperback edition 2020

Five Days in May

DEDICATION

To

The Vant Sant family and all those who suffered during the five years of Nazi occupation 1940-1945.

CONTENTS

1 The First Wave

2 Airborne Invasion of Waalhaven

3 Another Wave

4 In the Heart of The Maze

5 The River Mass

6 Light in Darkness

7 Rubble and Ruins

8 Rotterdam from the Sky

9 Resistance

10 The Knock

11 Tot Ziens

12 A Question of Time

13 Heroic Betrayal

14 Tilburg

15 A Good Scout

16 The River Meuse

17 The Red Tulip

Five Days in May

18 **The Crash**

19 **Back Down to Earth**

20 **Cracks on The Ceiling**

21 **The Seven Stars**

22 **The Hook of Holland**

23 **Staelduinse Forest**

24 **A New Dawn**

ACKNOWLEDGMENTS

My wife Kerry for her understanding and support. Our children Madeline, Rhianna and Rowan for accepting that their father's spare time had been dedicated to staring at a lap top (whilst I became immersed in this project). Many thanks to Warren Francis and Geoff Patch for their valuable comments on the early draft. Any remaining mistakes are entirely my own (and trust me, there will be mistakes). Finally, a special thank you to Madeline and Rhianna for helping with the design of the front and back cover.

Gary S Smith

CHAPTER ONE

THE FIRST WAVE

Five Days

"Friday, Saturday, Sunday, Monday and Tuesday. The bulk of another little nation is bashed and broken by brutal hands.

After five days of gallant fighting, five days of heroic resistance, northern Holland has been lost to Hitler. Pay tribute to the Dutch people. Peaceful people, who loved their land, but flooded and defiled it rather than choose an easy surrender.

Their five days' resistance may change the fate of the war. A nation which dies fighting will rise again."

[Extract from a British Newspaper 16th May 1940]

Approx. 0400, 10th May 1940, Waalhaven Airfield, South Rotterdam, Netherlands.

It was still dark when the first wave of bombs landed on Waalhaven airfield. The beauty of the pre-dawn bird song was replaced with a thunderous orchestra of ground

Gary S Smith

shaking explosions. In the barracks, Major Jansen screamed incoherent orders that created the necessary sense of urgency. Men cursed as they tried to get dressed in the dark. This wasn't a drill. Next came the clattering of boots along the wooden boards of the barrack room floor. Bleary eyed soldiers focused on the door. Kobus's eyes were open, but his body was still asleep. He pulled up his trousers in a pogo movement and threw on his jacket. Kobus had been in the army for two years, so he knew how to get into uniform quickly. But others were quicker. Kobus slipped his feet into his boots and staggered towards the door. His movement was restricted by his stiff legs, spread wide like a zombie. *The boot laces would have to wait.*

Suddenly an explosion shook the building. The blast knocked him sideways against the wall, or was it somebody else's flailing elbow. *Who could tell?*. It became an ugly scramble and it was every man for himself. A cloud of dust filled the room. "Get Out ! Get Out ! ….Now !" screamed Major Jansen. The men scrambled out of the barrack room door, partially dressed, clutching helmets and guns.

Outside the barracks there was mayhem. Some buildings next to the airfield were ablaze, including the massive Koolhoven factory. It was the factory that manufactured the fighter planes for the Dutch Airforce. At least one of the stationary aircrafts on the runway was engulfed in flames. Against the backdrop of burning buildings, shadowy figures were trying to operate water pumps towards the fire. The flames raged and pointed up to the sky, lighting up the pre-dawn darkness. The pilots sprinted to the far end of the runway, towards the stationary aircraft.

Jansen ordered his men into the burning buildings to salvage what they could and to search for wounded. This search didn't last long. A series of loud explosions reverberated from the adjacent Koolhoven factory. The flames inside the storage building had ignited a cocktail of ammunition cache's, resulting in a series of devasting explosions. The unlucky bastards inside the building had no chance. Two soldiers managed to stagger out of the building, engulfed in flames, but their screams could barely be heard above the mayhem. The human torches frantically rolled around on the grass trying to douse their burning bodies. Three nearby soldiers rushed in to help the burning men. They took off their jackets and tried to smother the flames. "Bring a stretcher!" somebody screamed, but it was too late for medical care.

The Koolhoven factory fire raged on as the heat inside the building intensified. Curious popping noises could be heard as shattered glass and shrapnel scattered around the building. The fire fighters backed off and kept their distance. The factory was now completely engulfed in flames. It was a lost cause. The unpredictable explosions from the ammunition stored within created chaos and fear to all those in the vicinity. Many soldiers ran for their lives into the darkness, onto the airfield and away from the burning buildings.

Kobus sprinted onto the runway and noticed a two metre wide bomb crater immediately in front of him. It was the only crater he could see on the runway, as most bombs seemed to have landed on or around the buildings. Nearby, a man was lying on his side on the ground. He had a pilot's jacket and was clutching a gas mask to his chest.
"Are you okay?" said Kobus, tapping the pilot on the back. He rolled him over to see his face. The pilot's face was black with soot and unrecognisable. His mouth was open, but no coherent words could be heard. The pilot's eyes glistened with hope and despair. Kobus crouched down beside him and noticed two medics close by, carrying a body on a stretcher.
"Wait there, don't move, we'll be back," said one of the

medics. The pilot tugged at Kobus's jacket. "Run. Get to the plane, get her airborne, quickly…." Kobus looked down at the pilot's bloody hand still clutching the inside of Kobus's jacket, and noticed that the pilots left trouser leg was missing, revealing a bloody stump ending just below the knee. "Okay, I'm going," said Kobus. He couldn't look at this awful sight anymore and he had to get away from him. In a state of appalling shock, he stood up and started to run towards the stationary fighter plane somewhere in the distance. At five feet nine inches tall, muscular build, Kobus was the ideal sprinter. He was the smallest out of his three brothers – *the little runt of the litter* had plenty of running practice.

Kobus strained his eyes in the murky light. Suddenly, he heard the sound of three or four other Fokker G.I. engines springing into life. It seemed that some pilots had driven along the airfield in cars to reach their aircraft, due to the distance of their location from their base. It was darker on this side of the runway, and this seemed safer than being near the blazing buildings. As Kobus got nearer to the end of the runway he saw other pilots running towards their planes clutching their oxygen masks.

Kobus's continued his run until he could see the outline of an aircraft in front of him. In the dim light of dawn he recognised, another pilot, Gert Van Der See, climbing into his cockpit. The Fokker G.I. engine started up with a judder and then the engine roared into life. It was an angry roar, the awakening of hope and revenge against the brutal attackers. Slowly his plane moved forward, and Kobus continued his run, now at jogging pace, looking for other planes, but they were all spread out. They had to save the fighter planes by getting them airborne before the German bombers picked them off like sitting ducks on the runway.

If there were not enough pilots alive, would Kobus fly? was Kobus

good enough to fly ?. Kobus was a trainee pilot - but had never actually flown a plane. He had flown in the Fokker G.I. three times but…. only as a passenger, and Kobus knew the plane controls and instruments but… only in theory. *Too many 'buts'.*
The noise of the nearby ignited engines on the ground, drowned out the sounds of the Heinkels above. This time many more bombs landed, mainly on the buildings and the trench positions that surrounded the airfield. One or two of the bombs landed on the airfield in a booming succession. Kobus dived onto the runway and placed both hands over his ears to block out the sound of deafening explosions. Dirt and stones rained down, landing on Kobus's back. Sergeant Kobus Van Hooten heard footsteps around him, as he now ran with the pack of pilots. For a moment he was one of *them*, a pilot. He shouted words of encouragement to the other pilots "Come on! keep going!". But by now all of the aircraft were manned with pilots. One by one, each fighter plane slowly moved forward and began to accelerate along the runway. As Kobus lay on the runway, panting heavily he watched the last plane take to the sky. It was a sense of relief, and pride that the twelve Dutch fighter planes could be unleashed to fight against the tide of the German airborne invasion.

He heard the heartfelt cheering from the Anti-Aircraft (AA) platoon positions around the runway. Kobus joined in, and for a moment there was hope. It was like watching the Feyenoord football team in the local De Kuip stadium. Kobus sat down cross-legged and reached for his cigarettes in his breast pocket. The packet was almost squashed. He pulled out a slightly bent cigarette and fumbled to strike a match quickly. As he exhaled the smoke through his nose, he looked up at the sky to the east. The rising sun was creeping through a row of trees in the distance. The yellow rays began to flicker across the airfield.

Suddenly the cheers faded from the Dutch positions, superseded by the distant rumbling noise from above. Kobus could see hundreds of the Heinkel bombers on the horizon, heading towards Waalhaven. The rumbling noise grew steadily louder, and Kobus stubbed out his cigarette under the sole of his boot he noticed that his boot laces were still untied. He looked around to take stock and it was only then that Kobus realised that he was the only person left on the runway.

Five Days in May

Gary S Smith

CHAPTER TWO

AIRBORNE INVASION

05.00 a.m. Sunday, 10th May 1940

Since the Napoleonic war, Rotterdam had been a city that lived in peace for 125 years. Peace had prevailed throughout World War One, due to the neutral status of the Netherlands. Despite the rising threat of Nazi Germany in the 1930's, it was expected that the Netherlands would once again remain "neutral."

In the 1930's, the Netherlands, just like Britain and France, had clung to the comfort blanket of appeasement. Due to the geographical misfortune of Hitler's Germany being a neighbour, the stakes were higher. Neutrality was understandable as there was no appetite to repeat the mass bloodshed of World War One which was still within living memory. The 1938 the expansion of Nazi Germany into Austria and Czechoslovakia were warning shots. Then the invasion of Poland in 1939 had provoked Britain and France into declaring war on Germany. The Dutch government still maintained neutrality. Hence, there was no reason to modernize its military capability. The army consisted of 200,000 poorly trained and ill equipped soldiers. Bicycles were used for transportation of troops, communication technology was not used (despite the presence of the Phillips company), and in May 1940 the

total number of tanks was…. zero.
In April 1940, the Nazis invaded Norway, and the Dutch Generals wrangled with politicians, but they still failed to agree on a coherent defence strategy. The Dutch had to fight any invasion with the tools that they had: which was not very much.

THE SECOND WAVE of bombers approached Waalhaven 5.00 a.m. It seemed bigger than the first wave. The Dutch Anti-Aircraft guns opened fire from their battery positions around the North and East of the Airfield. There was a huge L-shaped trench, that half surrounded the strategic airfield, where many sought refuge.

Feeling exposed, Kobus ran towards the nearest trench. Despite the semi-darkness, he knew its exact location, because he had helped to dig it. At the time of trench construction, it seemed like another pointless military exercise.

Kobus jumped feet first into the trench and accidently banged his elbow which spun him round as he fell to the bottom. He tasted the dirt as he lay face down. The bombs whistled down and exploded near the trench positions. The ground shook, and pieces of earth and concrete scattered around the field and some lumps came flying into the trench. The sound of flying shrapnel peppering the ground around the trench was unnerving. The smell of tar, soil and burnt metal filled the air. The terror was prolonged by the continuous intensity of the bombing. First came the whistling noise of the plummeting bombs, a two second silence, then the ear splitting boom. The worst part was the two second silence, it was as if the bomb was deciding on its target: *"no, not me,"* thought Kobus, *"please…. let it be somebody else."* The ground shuddered on impact, while dirt and debris continued to rain down into the trench. Immediately after the falling debris came an almighty deafening explosion from a bomb that was the closest yet. Kobus's eardrums reverberated, and he could hear nothing now, except a low buzzing sound. He was in a peaceful and dreamlike trance. A floating sensation emerged over him and he could only hear low muffled noises, as if he was swimming underwater. But right now, for Kobus that seemed like a good place to be.

THE SLIT TRENCH WAS DARK. Kobus could not hear what people were saying, only muffled shouts. The ground vibrated like an earthquake. When he finally removed his hands that were tightly pressed against his ears and rolled over in the trench he became aware that other troops were nearby, lying in similar positions, flat on their stomach's, faced down. Kobus realised that this wasn't just a personal experience, the nightmare was a shared experience.
Kobus felt a tremendously heavy object land on top of his back and it winded him. The unwelcome weight remained, pressing down on Kobus's lungs and against his rib cage. He couldn't breathe.
"Get off me you bastard, I was here first," said Kobus. It was a gut wrenching protest. There was no reply from above, just the warmth of a body on his back, and the heavy breathing on Kobus's neck. Next came a groaning apology "Kobus, it's me, Lars, err I mean Corporal Franssen!"
"Lars, you're lying on top of me, you idiot, crawl forwards!" said Kobus.
"Yes, Sergeant." Lars remembered to address Kobus by his rank as he crawled forwards scraping his boots across Kobus's back, until he got a foothold on Kobus's right shoulder and leapt forwards - boots clattering on Kobus's head in the process. This was a minor inconvenience, compared to the explosions above.
"Franssen? are you okay?" said Kobus, wiping dirt from

his mouth.

Lars spluttered, coughing drily "Yes, I think so, but I dropped my rucksack running across the airfield."

Kobus checked his gun. "I have a gun, but not much ammunition. Check your equipment."

As the sound of exploding bombs faded away, some people started to get on their knees and dust themselves down and shuffled around in the trench. There was some shouting for stretchers. The wounded and dead bodies were being pulled out the trench. It was a grim sight, and it was better not to look at the dead faces in case they were recognised. *"Death only happened to "other people." Thought Kobus.* The medics tended to the seriously wounded and began to stretcher people away. Some of the younger soldiers were clearly shell-shocked and began to desert their positions in small groups. They mingled in with the walking wounded and began to trudge away from the trenches towards the perimeter fence. The leaderless rabble was a sorry sight. Others sitting nearby were quietly gathering their weapons and ammunition and their shouts requesting more ammunition, but without reply. Kobus realised that he'd still not fastened his boot laces. Another man, kneeling in the trench, said "I picked up my gun ……..but I didn't have time to put my trousers on…"

The laughter had broken the tension, momentarily. The type of laughter that was driven by the nervous relief of surviving an attack. *So far, but what next?*.

Gary S Smith

CHAPTER THREE

ANOTHER WAVE

05.30 a.m. Sunday, 10th May 1940

There were still some dead bodies lay slumped on the floor of the trenches. The officers shouted for the men to spread out and remain in position, "hold firm!" shouted Major Jansen. They slowly stood up and raised their heads above ground level. Some rested their rifles on the grass, and the others followed suit. Ready and waiting. Beyond the black smoke that belched through the air, and the flickering flames on distant buildings, the dim light of dawn provided some more clarity on the extent of the devastation. Major Jansen had orders to destroy the remaining two Dutch fighter planes on the runaway. They could not leave these planes for the invading force.
"Men! disable the planes!."

Reluctantly the men took aim and fired their rifles. "I didn't join the army to shoot Dutch planes!" said Lars.
"…. I never even got to fly one," said Kobus as he aimed his rifle at the fuselage of the nearest Fokker. For some of the soldiers it was the first time they had ever fired live bullets.
Kobus was twenty-four years old and therefore older than most of his army colleagues. He had been still living at his

family home, and prior to joining the army he was studying to become a lawyer. It was a career path that had been firmly signposted by his father. After two years of day dreaming in lectures he became bored and restless. During his daily walk to university in Rotterdam, Kobus had seen a recruitment poster for the army. He made a spontaneous decision, driven by a simple quest for adventure.

Kobus wanted to become a pilot, but the Dutch Airforce was so small it fell under the command of the army. Aged twenty-two, he joined the aviation regiment in 1938 against the wishes of his parents. His father was a Calvinist preacher, and Sundays for Kobus's family were strictly for additional prayers and fasting. On this day there were no entertainments allowed including walking, cycling or hot meals. All of Kobus's three brothers had been guided along the middle class conveyor belt through university and then eased into professional occupations; doctors, teachers or lawyers. Kobus had rebelled and joined the army. His parents hadn't forgiven Kobus for his deviation, and the relationship with his father had become cold and distant. Two years later they seemed to have reluctantly accepted his folly and were politely curious of his adventures.

The sounds of sporadic rifle fire continued from the trenches until the two Dutch Fokker G.I.'s became burning wrecks. There were some craters on the runway, but most of the signs of bomb craters were concentrated around the perimeters of the airfield, where the battalions were located in the trenches with the heavy Anti-Aircraft guns.

"We need ammunition to fight these Germans, when they come back," said Private Bakker, who swept his blonde hair back with his soiled fingers.

"Most of the ammunition is in the burning buildings, creating a firework display. We need to share what we have left," said Major Jansen.

Medics ran across the runway and began shouting for

more help. The Major had other things on his mind.
"You'll be needing those bullets men. Look up at the sky," said Jansen.
The third wave arrived. Again, the sky was full of hundreds of German planes heading towards the air base. These Junker planes were bigger and slower, and they were flying very low. German Transport planes. The Dutch anti-aircraft guns began pounding the crowded sky which was provided many targets close together. Suddenly there was a shout to cease fire as half a dozen Dutch fighter planes were swooping down and firing at the Transport planes. The risk of hitting their own planes was too much. The Dutch were massively outnumbered in the air. It was a battle against the tides.

During the rise of Hitler's Germany, the Dutch command had invested two years of defence preparations building up "Fortress Holland" on the eastern side of the Netherlands. If the Germans invaded over the German/Dutch border the Dutch had planned to flood the dykes and create a giant waterfront of swamp land (from north to south) to slow down and entrap the attacking panzer divisions.
However, one month previously in April 1940 The Germans had attacked Denmark and Norway using large numbers of airborne troops. This created concern amongst the Dutch commanders and they reacted by placing Infantry battalions at the main ports and airbases at The Hauge, Ypenburg and the Waalhaven airfield, the latter in the south of Rotterdam on the island of Ijesselmonde. The Dutch troops had one month to prepare, and this was not enough time to train an under equipped part-time army.

The German Junker transportation planes were getting close now and flying low over the airfield at one hundred and fifty metres high. The Dutch AA platoons opened fire with their heavy Vickers AA guns, and the light weapons. There was a tremendous noise as several Junker planes burst into flames and crashed into the ground near the burning wreckage of Koolhoven.

Private Bakker was pointing up into the sky, pulled out his handkerchief to polish his glasses. He looked up again. There was no need for a third look.

"German Paratroopers!" shouted Bakker.

Many of the Dutch soldiers were also looking up at the semi-light sky, craning their necks. There was a cluster of white round canopies floating downwards.

The men on the ground stayed quiet and stared at the scene above them.

Slowly but surely the white objects in the sky became white canopies floating down towards the ground. They were everywhere. An alien invasion from another world. In May 1940, this mass parachute drop seemed like pure science fiction. The Dutch did not know this at the time, but they were the victims of the largest airborne invasion in history (so far).

"There's hundreds of them being dropped," said Lars.

"The Germans are trying to capture the airfield. They want the base for themselves," said Kobus.

German Paratroopers were floating down on top of the battalion over a one kilometer stretch. Major Jansen ordered his men to stay calm and take aim. They opened fire on the nearest parachutist before they could land.

At the same time a handful of Dutch fighter planes could now be seen swooping down on the German transport planes, which had begun to land on the airfield. They could hear the rat-tat-tat sound of the fighter plane guns. One of the Junkers was in flames, its tail fin trailing with smoke as it headed towards the perimeter fence. The cheers rippled along the trenches as the Junker broke into pieces as it crashed towards the ground.

"We got another one!" shouted Lars. There were obligatory cheers from the trenches, but many were preoccupied with the reality that the battle had moved from the sky to the ground. Hundreds of German stormtroopers landed on the ground, in front and behind the Dutch trenches.

Jansen's men opened fire and some Germans were falling down dead seconds after landing. Those landing nearby were shot down easily. Those landing further away, had some respite.

"Behind! they're attacking from behind," shouted Bakker.

Everybody could see that the German parachutist were now firing their pistols and advancing towards the trenches. Kobus heard a bullet whizz past his ear.

A paratrooper was running towards the trench ten metres away: getting closer. He raised his arm carrying a stick grenade like the Olympic flame. The paratrooper delayed his throw, to get nearer to his target, and brought his arm back like a baseball player about to bowl.

He was only five metres away now. Kobus's heart pounded as he shakily took aim, got him in his sights, pulled the trigger. His gun made a loud cracking noise and the German fell down, recoiling backwards, dropping his grenade in front of him. Kobus ducked instinctively.

"Grenade!" he screamed.

The explosion of the grenade sprayed clumps of dirt and shrapnel into the trench. Lars fell back clutching his face.

There was chaos everywhere. Above, planes above were shooting at each other, AA guns from the trenches pounded the sky. Bullets were flying around from light arms. The Dutch soldiers stopped shooting up above at the transport planes and parachutist because now it seemed that all of the Parachutist had now landed.

The initial sporadic charges of the invaders had failed. Dozens of Germans lay on the field, many had been shot either before they had even landed on Dutch soil, or in combat. The Dutch resistance had been stronger than the Germans expected. There was a pause in the battle. The Germans in front and behind seemed to regroup and were getting organised for an attack. Many more parachutists had landed, and they seemed to re-grouping and opening boxes of equipment. They had a plan.

"Lars, are you okay?" said Kobus, shouting above the sound of gun fire.

"..I don't know, I can't see out of my right eye… and my arm is sore…" Lars said quietly.

Kobus crouched over Lars, who was sat down in the trench clutching his arm. Two or three narrow lines of blood trickled from Lars's forehead down to his jawline.

"Let me look at your arm. Lars take your hand away, so I can see the wound," said Kobus.

When Lars slowly removed his shaking hand there was blood oozing from his left upper arm soaking his green uniform. Others crowded round, and Bakker was shaking his head in pity. "They got your head, but they missed your small brain," said Bakker. Lars forced a small grin, but that was it. At that moment Major Jansen was shuffling along the narrow trench, offering words of encouragement to the men.

"Sergeant Van Hooten, take Lars away from the trenches for urgent medical attention," said Major Jansen.

"Yes sir," said Kobus, looking round for medics.

"Head for the perimeter fence, and on the way…" the Major lowered his voice for discretion, "…try to make our boys hold their positions, firmly, in the trenches," said Jansen widening his eyes to enforce the words.

"Yes sir," said Kobus as Jansen moved his face even closer to Kobus.

"Our soldiers are young, and without experience and once a few of them retreat they will all collapse like a house of cards. Do you understand Van Hooten ?"

"Yes, sir, I will do my best to encourage them. What about the ammunition sir?" said Kobus

"There is none, use it wisely, and then use your knives…" said Major Jansen as he turned away to shout new instructions along the trench to his men.

"Hold your fire Bakker!, only shoot when they are in range!!" Shouted Major Jansen.

Kobus tore off part of his shirt tail and tied it round Lars's upper arm above the wound.

"Come on Lars, let's go," said Kobus.

They both shuffled along the trench, Kobus leading and the partially blinded Lars holding on to Kobus's coat from behind.

As they plodded along the trench, they could hear the battle raging on the south east side of the airfield. The Dutch soldiers fidgeted nervously awaiting the next German attack. Many were checking ammunition, and re-checking safety catches, counting bullets. Kobus could smell the fear in the trenches as he passed them by. One soldier was sitting down on the floor of the trench, legs crossed using both hands to cover his ears. He was visibility shaking. "Hey! soldier, stand up!" said Kobus.

The young soldier stood up slowly, staggering like a drunk. He looked no older than sixteen or seventeen, and his shirt sleeves were too long for him. "Yes, sir," said the soldier, making no eye contact with Kobus.

"Stay in the trench and stand behind the sandbags over there, and shoot any Germans that come near you, understand?" said Kobus.

"Yes, by I ...have.... never f-f-f-fired a gun before sir," said the soldier.

"You have been in training camp, yes?" said Kobus looking up to see another transport plane crash landing on the runway.

"J-j-just two weeks sir," said the young soldier, fidgeting nervously.

"Look, there are plenty of things to shoot at, just take care and don't shoot any Dutch soldiers. Keep your rifle resting on top of the trench, steady, then you can aim it straight," said Kobus.

"Okay sir, I'll try," said the soldier, but Kobus didn't hear the reply, due to the sounds of Anti-Aircraft gun fire nearby.

Eventually they climbed out the trench. There was no

medic in sight, so they moved away from the trenches and towards the main road. Some of the regiment leaving the battle scene were injured, helping to carry the injured. Others were unscathed and skulked away, quietly deserting their comrades.

Lars and Kobus stopped to rest under a small tree to adjust the makeshift bandage on Lars's arm. They looked over to the south east of the airfield where a fierce battle was in progress. A huge crowd of several hundred Dutch and the Germans were fighting head to head at close quarters. There were no battle lines or groups just one huge brawling mass of intermingled people; fist fighting, shooting, bayoneting. It was impossible to know if the screaming noises were battle cries of rage or cries of pain. It was a combination of the two. The Germans outnumbered the Dutch by two or three to one. It was a heroic defence.

The Dutch nation was twenty-five per cent lower than sea level, and throughout its history had defeated the waves of the ocean, by building dams, windmills and canals. On 10th May, the Dutch did not have the resources to push back the giant wave of German invaders.

Gary S Smith

CHAPTER FOUR

IN THE HEART OF THE MAZE

06.00 a.m. 10th May 1940

The airborne German paratroopers continued to fall from the sky attacking the Dutch trenches front and back. The battle remained chaotic and intense. The volume of Dutch gunfire was gradually reducing as the ammunition began to run out. Empty guns were being used as bayonets or batons in hand to hand combat. Under poor leadership, the troops were becoming a confused rabble. Individuals were just making their own personal decisions. *Fight to the last man?, surrender?, …or run?.*
For some brave souls, the choice was simple; those who no longer had ammunition surrendered to the Germans. Those who still had ammunition fought on until capture, or death.

Kobus sat in the trench next to Lars. Bullets whistled over their heads. Kobus could not leave Lars alone in his wounded state.
He looked at the blood soaked bandage from Lars's arm. "Let's hope the shrapnel went straight through the arm," said Kobus.
"I guess I'm lucky, it could be worse?" said Lars.
Kobus tied a new bandage around Lars's arm tightly.
"Cigarette?" said Kobus as he placed a cigarette into Lars's

mouth without waiting for an answer.
Just as Kobus struck the match, he instinctively ducked and dropped the match as he heard a grenade explode ten metres away and two Dutch soldiers fell backwards into the trench. Kobus, got to his feet and aimed his rifle at the advancing Germans, now within fifteen metres range. Suddenly a nearby Vickers machine gun post opened fire and quickly mowed down the entire group of tightly packed advancing Germans. Suddenly, on command, the Germans further back stopped their advance, and cautiously back-peddled towards cover. As they retreated the Dutch taunted the invaders.
"Dit is leuk!" shouted a young Dutchman, as he fired at the retreating Germans. The ironic gesture raised some laughs. This was the humour of the gallows, but everybody know there was no fun in death.

Kobus struck a match to light his own cigarette, and then lit up Lars's cigarette. Kobus noticed that his own hand was shaking. He took a large drag and exhaled the smoke from his nose and mouth simultaneously.
The Dutch soldier who had shouted the gesture, was now out of ammunition, and for sure, the fun had stopped. He wandered over towards them behind the trench. The soldier was tall, lanky, and had several shirt buttons were undone. His helmet was missing.
"Do you have any ammunition?" he said frantically.
"Sure, take this," said Kobus as he passed over Lars's rifle and ammunition belt. It was an old Austrian rifle from 1890.
"Get one of the Nazis…. for Lars," said Kobus.
"Yes sir," said the soldier as he grabbed the rifle and ran along the trench, to his position.
Kobus's stubbed out his cigarette on the hard grassy ground.
Lars's face was looking pale. He was losing blood.
"Lars? we have to move now," said Kobus.

Five Days in May

"How far, until we get to the ambulance?" said Lars.
"Not far," said Kobus, being optimistic and saying the right things. More bullets fizzed over their heads, as they shuffled along the trench, Lars was walking slowly in front, unaided, but under the watchful eye of Kobus who followed behind like a shadow. Progress was steady but too slow.

As they moved along the German voices could be heard advancing now, and throwing their stick shaped grenades with more frequency, and accuracy. Grenades that landed in tightly packed trenches were proved devastating. The Dutch had not been issued with grenades and had not seen the effects of this weapon before. More Dutch soldiers surrendered in groups, and several troops could be seen abandoning the battlefield and running towards the perimeter fence.

Kobus paused for breath after carrying Lars piggy back style along the trench.
"Lars, you're heavy. What's your mother feeding you on?"
"Milk……cheese… bread," said Lars, as if he was reading from a shopping list.
"Milk…typical Dutchman," said Kobus.
"Yes," said Lar's as he held on to the lip of the trench, swaying slightly.
"Do you think I'll be okay Sergeant Van Hooten?"
"I don't know, I'm not a doctor," said Kobus, speaking with the calmness of a doctor. Kobus looked behind to see large groups of Germans advancing into the trench location where they had just lit up their cigarettes.
"We have to move to the perimeter fence, before we are taken prisoner, or shot," said Kobus.
Lars squinted in the distance.
"It's about five hundred metres, can you make it if we get out of the trench and cut across the field?" said Kobus.
"Yes sir," said Lars.

"We stay low, and move quick, no stopping this time, understood?"

Before Lars could answer, Kobus climbed out of the trench and pulled Lar's up from his arm pits and hoisted him onto the field, Kobus placed his arm around Lars's back and push him forward.

"Now! run!". They ran for fifty metres and stopped behind a gun position protected by a semi-circle of sandbags. The battlement was full of Dutch troops, either manning the huge machine gun or taking pot shots at the Germans with their rifles.

Kobus paused for breath. The large Skoda machine gun post still being held by the Dutch infantry. They also had a Vickers machine gun, with boxes of ammunition being ripped open. The gunners were firing away "rat-tat-tat-tat". The gun crew were feeding the ammunition belt into the machine gun. They were surrounded by five or six riflemen who were firing in all directions; front, behind and sideways, protecting the position. It slowly dawned on Kobus that he was the most senior ranking soldier present.

"Sergeant are we fighting well?" said a young soldier, whose faced was riddled with teenage spots. He was no more than eighteen years old, short sleeves, with his jacket missing.

"Yes. Like typical Rotterdammer's. You are tough, stubborn and getting on with the job," said Kobus proudly.

"What's your name?" said Kobus.

"Private Van Der Clerk, sir" said the spotty teenager as he fired his rifle.

"Have you any wounded soldiers who need moving?" asked Kobus.

"Not now, our men took them to the medics tent near the perimeter fence," said the spotty teenager reloading his gun with a cool efficiency.

"Over there," said Van Der Clerk, pointing to a small tent near the large two metre tall perimeter fence.

Five Days in May

"Okay, thanks, that's about five hundred metres away…cover us and keep firing," said Kobus as the Vickers machine gun burst into life.

"Lars, can you sprint?" said Kobus putting his rifle strap around his back.

"I'll try, but still cannot see properly…."

"1, 2, 3, Let's go Lars! - now!" They both ran out into the open field going diagonally away from the machine gun post. They were exposed. No cover on the flat field. Fortunately, the Vickers machine gun kept on pelting out bullets toward the Germans who were busily trying to out flank the machine gun. Kobus and Lars ran, heads down across the field, Kobus slightly in front of Lars who was holding his wounded arm, but he was moving much better now. All was going well until Lar's let out a cry and fell.

"Ughh!" grunted Lars as he fell to the ground. Kobus stopped in his tracks and jumped on the ground next to Lars.

"Are you hit!" said Kobus.

"No, I tripped over something! it was a body," said Lars.

"Oh, good. Well…you know what I mean.." said Kobus.

They started again, this time the perimeter fence was in sight, they passed several white parachutes lying on the floor rippling in the gentle morning breeze. They plodded through the fresh green grass that was slightly longer here. All of a sudden there was a movement in the grass to their right.

"Halt!" shouted a voice, followed by the crack of a rifle. Lars's fell to the ground. Kobus jumped down on top of Lars. He rolled his limp body over so that Lars was facing up. Lars's forehead was covered in blood. Lars's eyes had a fixed stare. A frozen expression of death. He had been killed instantly. Kobus wriggled onto his stomach. Burning with anger, and then he was pulling his rifle strap off his back, to get into a firing position. Kobus looked up, at the barrel of the Schmeisser submachine gun, within three feet of his face. His heart skipped a beat in terror as his

moment of death had arrived. The German pulled the trigger, but nothing happened except the dullest of clicking sounds.
Kobus was still lying on the floor and swung his old Austrian rifle upwards at the German's chest and he squeezed the trigger, the loud cracking noise seemed to echo across the field, as the paratrooper fell down to his knees clutching his stomach, eyes bulging. He was still alive. Kobus got to his feet and this time *he* was standing over the German. Kobus swung the butt of his rifle downwards like an axe. It made a dull cracking noise as it smashed into the back of the Paratroopers neck. "Bastard. Lars was wounded, and you still shot him," spat Kobus, almost waiting for an answer. The German leaned slowly forward and slumped to the ground.
Then Kobus went back to Lars to check his pulse, but avoided looking at the face of his dead comrade. He was definitely dead.

For a moment Kobus crouched in the field on his knees and looked around to see if his altercation with the German had attracted any attention. The Dutch positions were now being encircled by hundreds of German Parachutist. He could no longer hear the sound of the heavy Vickers guns. The shouting noises were increasing on the field of battle. It was mainly shouting of German commands, who seemed to be everywhere. The Vickers machine gun petered out. Kobus could see a white flag in the distance and Dutch voices were desperately pleading for surrender, but the shots continued amidst the shouts of protest.
Kobus realised that he had to escape quickly from the gloom of the encircling net. He continued to run for the perimeter fence or *would he go for the river?*. He was a like a rat trying to find his way out from the heart of the maze.

Five Days in May

Gary S Smith

CHAPTER FIVE

THE RIVER MAAS

"Everything is out in the open. No mountains, no caves. Nothing to hide. No dark places in the soul." (Cees Nootboom, Dutch novelist).

06.30 a.m. 10th May 1940

Kobus ran across the field towards the perimeter fence, glancing around from side to side like a hunted animal. Initially, the distance seemed around two hundred metres away. In reality it was further away, due to the disorientating flat terrain. Maybe it was four hundred metres. Kobus began to blow and pant as he tried to maintain his speed, stooping lower to reduce his target size for German snipers. He sprinted across the grass arching his back, in a peculiar crouching run.
After a while, his posture became upright again, as the need for speed took precedence over cover. The terrain was flat, open field, with only a few sticks like trees (a typical Dutch landscape). He was exposed and vulnerable. Kobus increased his pace, feeling the adrenalin, like a hunted rabbit at dawn. His senses were heightened, listening intently for the anticipated sound of a sniper's gun.
As he plodded through the next farmer's wheat field, it was waist high, Kobus felt subconsciously less exposed, at least he could dive into the grass for cover. He had

managed to move away from the perimeter fence and was heading towards the river. It seemed like a safer route. There was a buzzing noise above of a small aircraft, and he looked up at the sky. The vast blue sky was almost cloudless. Only a smattering of planes and small white puffs of anti-aircraft flak. Suddenly, high up above he craned his neck. Yes, it was a fighter plane. A lone Dutch Fokker G1 fighter heading towards Waalhaven. His eyes were transfixed on the lone aircraft flying towards the Nazi occupied Waalhaven, but he didn't slow down, heading for the river now. In the distance to the south there were small groups of retreating Dutch soldiers leaving the airbase heading south. He knew they were Dutch because of their rounded helmets.

To the North and the East, the white canopies of German parachutes continued to land in large numbers. However, the south seemed clear, for now. Now that Lars had been killed, he had no need to go to the medical tent. As an officer and a trainee pilot he would be taken in by the Germans as a prisoner of war. *But where should he go now? join up with the nearest Dutch unit?*. Firstly, he had to cross the River Maas, to get off the occupied island.
Kobus trotted slowly now, heart pounding, breathing heavily. Two Kilometers away from Waalhaven airbase, and now he could smell the river. He made towards a pine tree, and as he got near he noticed a large ditch behind the tree. Standing on the edge he was just about to jump in feet first, when he saw two men pointing rifles at him.
"Don't shoot!" said Kobus.
The two soldiers were part of the Dutch regiment attached to the airbase. (*Although they were not very attached now*).
Sergeant Dirk Van Klooster was in mid-twenties, dark hair slicked back, his group of men had surrendered when their trench was swamped with Germans. In the confusion, Dirk made a run for it with Corporal Wilhelm Smit. Kobus knew Dirk and Smit from the army camp. Now they were

all in the same boat.

"The battle is *over* Kobus, they have taken over the airbase and the Dutch are either dead, wounded, surrendered or on the run," said Dirk, now smoking one of Kobus's cigarettes. Smit was sat at the top of the ditch keeping lookout. He was resting his rifle onto the grass and lying down in a sniper position.

"What now?" said Kobus wiping the sweat from his forehead.

"We can die like martyrs," said Dirk pointing back to the airbase, "or join another regiment," pointing loosely in the other direction.

"I agree. We will have to a find another regiment," said Kobus.

"If we head south, we might meet some Dutch or maybe French reinforcements," said Dirk.

"Wearing an army uniform? if the Germans see us, they will shoot us, so we may as well fight to the death," said Smit, who had put down his rifle and was now sharpening a stick with his army knife. Smit looked very youthful, tall, thin and had a mop of blonde hair. He hadn't quite "filled out" yet so his uniform looked a bit baggy. But he seemed confident. Perhaps over confident.

"Not with four bullets….and a sharp stick," said Dirk sarcastically. Kobus laughed, and Smit's cheeks flushed in anger.

"Let's go now, before the Germans find us," said Dirk, standing up showing urgency.

Five Days in May

Dirk and Kobus left the ditch and began walking quickly towards the River Maas. Smit stabbed his stick into the ground and picked up his rifle. He followed reluctantly, as he was disappointed that his proposal to stay and fight had been firmly rejected by Dirk, without serious consideration. Dirk sensed Smit's disappointment and put his arm around Smit's shoulders.
"You're a good scout Smit, stay with me and you'll be okay. You might even win a medal or become an officer one day," said Dirk. The pep talk seem to sooth Smit's darkening mood.
"Yes, Sergeant Van Klooster," said Smit drily.
As they approached the river they walked more slowly and began to crouch in anticipation.

"Wait!" said Dirk. "There is something not right here."

All three stopped still. There was no breeze, the river was narrow at this point, around ten metres wide and was moving slowly, glistening under the morning sun. there was peculiar silence.

They tentatively walked along the bank until they spotted an old man in a fishing boat. The boat had a sky blue base and a small white cabin. The name painted in black letters on the side of the boat was "Selene". The old man , had a white beard, glasses, and a flat cap. He was busy filling his pipe with tobacco. He saw them approach and looked up, unsurprised.

"Goedenmorgen!" said Dirk. "Please take us across the river," said Kobus.
The old man nodded and spread out one arm as a sign of invitation. The three men carefully stepped into the boat and sat down.

"How do I know you are not fifth columnist?, NSB,

Nazis," said the old man as he started up the engine and spun the boat round to cross over the canal.

Dirk laughed.
"You won't find any Dutch Nazis on Waalhaven at the moment, it's full of *real* Nazis. You'll just have to take our word for it, Waalhaven has fallen and we need to join up with the reinforcements," said Dirk.

The old man slowly nodded as if he knew already.
"Okay, but I'll tell you something. I've been out fishing since dawn and the Germans have taken the nearby bridges over the Maas, and there are rumours of fifth columnist dressing up in Dutch army uniforms. I have taken many soldiers across the river. Everybody is escaping from Waalhaven."

"Have you seen any Dutch reinforcements?" said Smit.
"No, but on the radio they say the Germans have landed in the Hague and Rotterdam. The River is not safe further up towards the City. They are taking the bridges."

"Okay, just take us to the other side, then and we'll find our way to the coast." said Kobus.
"Why is your boat called *Selene,* is that your lady friend?" said Smit inquisitively.
The old man looked around at Smit, as the boat cruised gently to the other side.
"For a young man, you ask personal questions!" said the old man.
Smit just smiled, and said nothing.
"The coast?, that is at least one full day's walk," said Dirk.
"Any other ideas, Dirk?" said Kobus.
"Not at the moment, let's head North-West towards the coast and see what happens, we might meet up with reinforcements. I don't want to leave Rotterdam. My daughter lives here, and I need to check she is safe."

Five Days in May

Kobus nodded, showing his understanding. He did not ask about Dirk's wife. Kobus had family in Rotterdam, but he wanted to become a pilot more than anything else in the world. In reality it was an opportunity for Kobus to go anywhere.
On the other side of the Maas, the men thanked the old man.
"Dank u wel," said Smit. Dirk handed the old man a packet of Lucky Strike cigarettes before stepping off the boat.
"Wees Voorzichtig," said the old man who raised his hat to reveal a huge bald patch.
"By the way, the boat is named after my Granddaughter, *Selene*, said the old man, but when he looked up the three men had already began walking away from the canal towards quieter roads that were out of view of the river and the bridges. They were local Rotterdammers, so they knew the back roads. As they walked, Kobus began to *weigh up* his new companions.

Sergeant Dirk van Klooster, had a smart appearance, neat combed back black hair and an athletic build. He was organised, and was well suited to military life. At age 27, Klooster had plenty of confidence and experience of discipline and authority under his belt. He was a former policeman, so he blended into the army very easily.

Smit was very young, and had joined the army straight from school, and naturally looked up to Klooster. However, they couldn't have been more different personalities. Smit was outspoken, but naïve and lacked experience. Even Smit's hair was so blonde it was almost white; Dirk's hair was so dark he was almost black.

As they silently walked through a small village, a cloud of black smoke could be seen rising in the distance. Anti-

Aircraft flak guns rumbled in the distance, and small clouds of flak peppered the sky. They could still smell the Smoke from the Waalhaven base as they walked in a westerly direction. Then it became clear that the smoke was also coming from the City. Sounds of sporadic gunfire could be heard in the distance. They began to walk single file and closer to the thick wall of hedge rows, that lined the country lane.

Smit handed around his water cannister to his two companions. There was a silence as each person was in deep thought. *What should they do next?, fight?, hide?, surrender? or just go home change into civilian clothes and check on the family?.*

"Okay, Dirk. Anymore thoughts. Where do you want to go?, Rotterdam port, back to Waalhaven, or to go home?" said Kobus.

"I can't leave Rotterdam, until I know my daughter is safe. But I'm not going back to Waalhaven to be captured as a prisoner," said Dirk in a low voice.
"I saw them shoot some of the Dutch soldiers who tried to surrender," said Smit as he hooked his water cannister back on his belt.
"*Surrender* sounds like a bad option," said Kobus. "I'm thinking of heading to the coast, so I can join reinforcements, or if there aren't any, then I'll take a boat to England, before the Germans take over the port," said Kobus.
As they spoke more German transport planes filled the sky flying low overhead towards Waalhaven. They instinctively increased their walking pace.
"I'll go with Dirk," said Smit, still sulking from Dirk's dismissal of Smit's earlier proposal.
Dirk took off his round Dutch helmet and ran a hand through his hair. It was becoming a warm day, and his dark shiny hair was wet with perspiration.

Five Days in May

"I think we will head towards the coast together and see if we meet reinforcements on the way. We'll get a better idea the further along the road we go," said Dirk

"It's a plan," said Kobus.

The three comrades continued to walk. They could have been soldiers from a by-gone age: with their old fashioned round helmets and their 1890 Austrian rifles slung over their shoulders.

Gary S Smith

CHAPTER SIX

LIGHT FROM DARKNESS

February 1942 – Squires Gate, England

Nearly two years after the attack on Waalhaven Airfield, Kobus Van Hooten had fulfilled his dream of becoming a pilot. Except it was not the Dutch Airforce, but the British RAF. Kobus had escaped from Rotterdam to England by boat on 15th May 1940. After three months of internment in Bristol, he had joined the Dutch brigade whilst applying for a flying officer position with the RAF. Now, he had been training to be a pilot for almost one year. Most pilots were British, but there were also Canadian, French, Polish and Dutch pilots.
Britain was the only unoccupied country in Europe and all of Kobus's fellow students had one thing in common. They all wanted to become RAF pilots to fight the Nazis.

Kobus was sat in a large wooden hut with twenty three other trainee pilots. All of the trainees in the Photographic Reconnaissance Unit (PRU) were training to fly Spitfires over occupied France, Belgium, Netherlands and Germany. The whole purpose was to take aerial photographs of strategic German military locations such as dockyards, battleships locations, weapons factories, V-Rocket bases and post bombing analysis. The secret photographs taken by the RAF would then be handed to the British intelligence services, who could then use this information to plan future bombing targets and military operations.

Flight Lieutenant Stevenson stood up at the front of the class, rocking forwards on his toes to emphasize his status as the training officer. He wore an immaculately pressed blue uniform with RAF wings sown on to his blazer jacket. Stevenson looked and sounded like the stereotypical RAF pilot with slicked back hair and the classic BBC accent. The bryl-creem black hair shined in the light from the uncovered light bulb on the low ceiling of the wooden hut.

"Now, listen here men. The planes you fly will be different to all other planes in the RAF. The good news is that these Spitfires will be a single seater small machine that fly high enough to avoid AA fire from the ground which is 30-40,000 feet. Its sheer speed and climbing ability make it the fastest plane in our service."

"Sir, is it faster than the German Fw190 or the ME109?" asked Flying Officer Porter.

"You'll soon find out," said Flight Lieutenant Stevenson. There was ripple of laughter around the room. It was a nervous laughter.

Stevenson continued. "The bad news is that there are no guns on this plane, and no radios. The good news is that without this *extra baggage*, the plane is lighter and therefore faster. There is also more room for fuel, especially with its deeper chin for extra fuel storage…so you can fly for longer…. say to …. Germany and back for example. The planes are fitted with F24-5inch focal length camera on each wing. The cameras point vertically down and go off at the same time. The entire objective is to take photographs, get back to England in *one piece* and hand them photos to the intelligence people. Job done. Bravo."

Five Days in May

Flying officer Van Hooten raised his hand. "Sir, how fast can we fly?."

"Around, 390 mph. In the Spitfire PR Mark IV you will climb faster than the ME109, and if you stay high, you have a good chance of evading enemy aircraft. The Spitfire PR Mk IV will turn faster than any German fighter plane".

Stevenson took a large gulp from his cup of tea. "Now then, where was I ? So if you get jumped by a German fighter plane, turn, turn and turn. Lots of quick turns to shake him off your tale".

Kobus looked around at Gordon and Porter, and there was a nervous excitement in the room. A white knuckle ride awaited them.

"Your aircraft has a PRU blue camouflage colour underneath the wings for high altitude and if for low altitude flights we have something different. The actual colour is a matter of … erm debate, blue-green…. maybe even…pink?. The RAF call it "Camotint".
There was a pause whilst the flying officers debated the colour amongst themselves.
This gave Lft. Stevenson a chance to have another sip of his precious tea.
Flying officer Peter Gordon slowly raised his hand.
"Yes, Gordon?"
"Sir, for the purposes of my understanding. We fly alone, 35,000 ft high, 700 miles over occupied Europe to Germany and back, in a *pink* Spitfire with a big chin, no guns, no radios… and we come back with photographs?"

"Bravo!. Welcome to the PRU, Gordon! …and that's all for today gentlemen. I'll see you all tomorrow morning 8 a.m. sharp," said Stevenson.

Gary S Smith

Van Hooten and most of the other flying officers retreated to the comforts of the Pub, the White Hart. Room temperature ale, good chatter amongst the pilots, darts, and …more ale. Kobus was enjoying his life in England.

***

The training continued the next day, in the same room. There was a lot of information to remember. The pilots just wanted the training to end so they could get into the aircraft and fly.

Stevenson began to go through his checklist of important training tips.
"Now listen men," said Stevenson in his authoritative tone, pointing his cane at the blackboard which was dominated by a long list.

"No. 1 Met Report
STUDY your MET report carefully. Work out the wind speed and direction to calculate an accurate course. Study the weather not just over the target area but in and out of the route.
No. 2 - Trails.
You will see in your report the height at which you are likely to leave trails. You will find out from experience that you nearly always leave a trail if you fly near the base of High Cirrus cloud.
If you trail over a target enemy flak and fighters know your *exact* position. But if you go up to trail height over a safe area on your way to the target and note the *exact height* at which you commence to leave a trail you can use the knowledge to your own advantage, if you fly 500 to 1,000 ft BELOW TRAIL HEIGHT any ENEMY FIGHTERS above you WILL LEAVE A TRAIL. You can easily spot this and lessen your chances of being JUMPED."

Five Days in May

Flight Lieutenant Stevenson took a large gulp from his mug of tea, and as he lifted his cup, he exposed a small round wet patch around his arm pit.

"No. 3 Petrol Consumption
In order to carry out successful operations in this unit it is ESSENTIAL that you have a THOROUGH KNOWLEDGE of the petrol consumption of your aircraft. You will have to carry out long trips at times which, although you have adequate petrol to complete them safely, you will NOT have enough to allow for errors in navigation, too many runs over the target and flying at low altitude, etc. if you go badly off course for any reason TURN BACK. If the target area is covered in medium or low cloud, DON'T fly under it. TURN BACK. It's better to be a LIVE pilot without photographs than a DROWNED one with them. There is nothing more DISGRACEFUL than to go into the SEA, or land in enemy territory through making an error in your calculations and RUNNING OUT OF PETROL.... UNDERSTAND ?.."

"YES, SIR !!" echoed the class in unison. Running out of petrol seemed like a bad idea at 35,000 ft.

"No. 4 Cockpit Check
Before you climb into the cockpit, check the chocks are in position.
The cleaver should be in cold air and oil pressure relief valve is CLOSED.
When you're in the cockpit TURN OVER YOUR CAMERAS.
SEE THAT YOUR HOOD CLOSES properly.
TURN ON YOUR OXYGEN and check that its working satisfactory.

No. 5 Other points
When you are in range of an enemy fighter, KEEP WEAVING, it's your own fault if you are JUMPED. THE Blisters are not put on the aircraft for decoration.
 REMEMBER you are a RECONNAISSANCE PILOT. Keep your eyes open for all types of enemy movement, shipping, aircraft, tanks, etc., both on your way out to and from the target area."

Van Hooten looked outside the window at a Spitfire taking off on the runway. When he looked around, the entire classroom was staring out of the window at the same thing. They admired the curves and the beauty of the machine. She was majestic and stylish, a work of art.

"It's the new model of Spitfire," said Stevenson, "Apparently, *she's a beauty*. Just the ticket."

Five Days in May

Gary S Smith

CHAPTER SEVEN

RUBBLE AND RUINS

Through foreign violence in dust and ash. I arose more beautiful than I will ever be. (anon)

08.00 a.m. 12th August 1942, Rotterdam,

The morning sun was dominant against Rotterdam's skyline which had been reduced to rubble. The brightness of the new day only highlighted the ugliness of the city. The absence of the tall buildings opened the door to a cool wind that Rotterdammers knew only too well. Despite the destruction of many of the city's buildings the grit and determination of Rotterdammers had ensured that life would continue, as best as possible. They had to make the most of what resources they had. After all, what other choice did they have?.
During the capitulation of the Netherlands in May 1940, Dirk Van Klooster along with Wilhelm Smit had decided to stay in Rotterdam, whereas Kobus set off to the coast to escape to England. *Who could blame him?*. Today, Dirk was taking his five year old daughter Helen to school. They walked hand-in hand along the one kilometer journey, watching the swirling clouds of powdered dust skimming across the piles of rubble onto road. Dirk looked smart in

his dark brown suit and white shirt. It fitted him better than his Dutch army uniform, which was no longer needed. Nowadays, any fighting against the Nazis, was done without uniform, in civilian clothes. Dirk was now part of the underground resistance. He stopped to cough into his handkerchief. *Bloody dust!*. They started walking again. Previously they had both cycled to school. The reason they were both walking to school today was because yesterday his bicycle had been stolen by a German soldier. There was no point in reporting the theft to the local police station, because the police chief was a member of the Dutch fascist party, the NDS. As far as NDS were concerned the German soldiers could never be guilty of stealing anything from the Dutch people. Besides, Dirk did not want to draw attention to himself. Helen's blonde pig tails bounced on her shoulders as she tried to skip along despite the constraints of her father's clutching hand. Her clean blue dress seemed to reflect the morning sun. The city was a bomb site and it was no place for a child to live.

"Helen, can you stop kicking the dust?. I've only just polished your shoes this morning and they were shiny black. Now they are grey," said Dirk.
"But Dad, the dust is like magic, it blows everywhere!" said Helen. Only a child could discover magic in such a grim setting.
"I know Helen, but just be careful, and don't go climbing on the piles of rubble."
"…. But Dad, they are just like small mountains,"
"*But Helen*, The Netherlands is flat. There are no mountains here, nor in Eindhoven where Grandma and Grandad live" said Dirk. Dirk had spoken to Helen that morning informing her that she would be going to live in Eindhoven with her Grandparents. She had cried, but Dirk assured her that it would be temporary until the war was over. Nobody knew when the war would be over.

Gary S Smith

The road to school was clear of civilian traffic. Most civilian cars had been requisitioned by the Nazis. People walked or used their bikes. Both sides of the road had been reduced to rubble during the bombing of Rotterdam in May 1940 and had remained that way for the past two years. Some of the rubble had been cleared and thrown into the nearby canals and rivers. The only prominent landmark building still left standing was the cathedral. The remains of its ravaged tower pointed accusingly up at the sky. The culpable party was beyond all reasonable doubt.

14th May 1940 was the day when the German bombers had flattened Rotterdam. The mass bombing had created a huge fire that swept across the city. The fire brigade had no water to control the fire because the water mains has been damaged during the bombing. Therefore with the aid of a breeze, perfect conditions were created for a heat so intense, that some fires still burned three months after. The bombing was a cruel ultimatum to force the Netherlands to surrender and avoid its other cities being destroyed in the same way. The tragic irony was that despite the day the Dutch agreed to surrender, hundreds of German bombers were already on their way and failed to abort their mission to destroy the city. The scale of the devastation is difficult to comprehend. 80,000 homes were destroyed, 500 cafes, 12 cinemas, 21 churches. Miraculously only 2,000 were recorded as dead.

Helen's school had been one of the 70 schools bombed, so they were using the local church as an alternative venue. It was the type of practical solution that many civilians were forced to take. People carried on with their daily lives clinging to the comfort of some form of normality. Since May 1940, Dirk had been working at the ticket office at the railway station in Rotterdam. However, fewer trains were running nowadays as most of the rolling stock had been taken away from the Netherlands and moved to the

Five Days in May

Eastern front in Russia to support German troop movements. The result was that Dirk was only needed on a part-time basis. Dirk had spare time on his hands. Time to support the Dutch underground resistance movement.

Before Dirk had dropped Helen off at the church school, he gave her a kiss, handed her a bag of sandwiches and waved goodbye. Helen's grandma would collect Helen later and take her to Eindhoven where there was a proper school, it was safer, and it was away from the rubble and ruins of Rotterdam.
Helen's mother, Emily, had died of polio a couple of years before war. Dirk had never really recovered from the tragic loss of the love of his life. For the first few months after her death Dirk was overcome with a gut wrenching sadness. Gradually a year later he emerged into a state of emotional emptiness. Dirk would never forget her radiant smile and her infectious sense of humour. Emily was a natural mother, and what should have been, a guaranteed life partner. Sometimes Dirk felt as if she had been stolen from him, and other times he bitterly accepted the cruel luck of health and survival. Nowadays he could only love the memory of Emily. Occasionally he would sit in his house with a glass of whiskey and look at a small photograph of Emily. Even though it was black and white, but he could still see her piercing blue eyes, and her bright cherry lips. Her silky blonde hair tied back revealed her smooth cheeks, and long elegant neck. Sometimes after too many whiskeys he would talk to the photograph as if she was still alive.

Dirk met up with Smit outside the bakery at 0830, as arranged. Smit was wearing flat cap, shirt sleeves rolled up above the elbows, black loose fitting trousers and workman's boots. Smit was standing in the queue for the Bakery shop, smoking a cigarette. The queue that trailed out onto the pavement and alongside the neighbouring pharmacy shop. Dirk recognized the distinctive bald head, and prominent nose of a man called Van De Raal, who was nicknamed "De Rat". De Rat was always talking to the Germans. The Germans relied on "Informers" to receive information about the resistance. Dirk and Smit were convinced that De Rat was an informer.

"Hoe Gaat Het Met U ?" said Dirk, in a low voice.
"Het Gaat Goed," said Smit as he stubbed out his cigarette on the floor and folded his newspaper under his arm.
Dirk cocked his head towards the De Rat.
"Wees Voorzichtig," said Dirk.
"De Rat is here," said Dirk as he turned slowly to walk down the street. They both began walking, but there was no talking as they walked, Nearby, stood in the middle of street stood were two Germans who were staring at a young Dutch girl in the queue outside the Bakery, slathering like hungry dogs as the morning breeze made her skirt ascend to entertain the watching eyes. It was as if it was the first time they had seen a young woman's legs before.

Half way down the street, Dirk began to talk business.
"I have another delivery for *Selene*. More fish, that need to be released along the Maas, into the Sea," said Dirk.
"Oh yes, what type ?" said Smit.
"Two adults and one child. Each with a yellow stripe"
"Where from? a good hiding place," said Smit.
"Yes, but the less you know the better, we don't want to get our comrades into trouble. They are taking a lot of risk hiding Jews in their houses," said Dirk.
"We are *all* taking risk, the Gestapo will torture us and kill us for this," said Smit, who stopped walking now and was facing Dirk.
Smit momentarily showed concern as he rubbed his half-shaven chin. He looked up to the sky seeking an answer,

Five Days in May

blinking as he faced the sun. Then he looked at Dirk and smiled.
"The bastards have to catch us first," said Smit.
"We need to be careful, keep your head down Smit, don't tell *anybody anything*, and don't take stupid risk," said Dirk.
"I know, I know, but so far so good," said Smit.
"That is why we cannot recruit people. Most people won't take the risk of smuggling Jews out of the Netherlands," said Dirk.
"I know, it's not an easy decision, but we also know that our friends and fellow citizens are being sent to camps, and we never see them again," said Dirk.
"That's why we need a bigger boat to get more people out of the Netherlands to somewhere safe," said Smit, who once again impatiently rubbed his blond stubble on his chin. He was waiting for Dirk's approval.
"That sounds too risky. We can talk about this another time," said Dirk dismissively.
Smit did not say anything. He swallowed in disappointment. His ideas were *always* shot down by Dirk.
Dirk had seemed to forget that it was Smit's idea to use the old man's fishing boat (Selene) to smuggle Jews along the canal to the port of Rotterdam.
"This time we are lucky that the hiding place is quite near to where your boat is docked. We will walk along the river in our fisherman clothes and fishing rods, before dawn. We will reach your boat at 2.00a.m tomorrow morning. If we are not there by 2.15 a.m. just go, and abort the mission," said Dirk, hands in pockets.
"…and there's a curfew in place after 8pm so we could get arrested, so remember to wear black clothes," said Dirk
"We could go at dawn?" said Smit
"But if we go at dawn, at first light it's easier to get spotted," said Dirk.
"Okay, let's stick to *your* plan. Meet at 2.00 a.m." said Smit reluctantly.
"I'll see you later, good luck," Dirk winked and forced a

smile. At that moment a half shaven Smit looked much older than the fresh faced young soldier of May 1940.
"Take care, happy fishing," said Dirk, as they reach the corner of the road. Dirk turned left, and Smit turned right.

Smit had the feeling that he was being followed but resisted the temptation of turning around to check. Being in the resistance meant that acting *normally* was an essential smokescreen to avoid suspicion.

Ever since the old man with the white beard (who they had first met on 10th May 1940) had agreed to loan his small boat to help them smuggle Dutch Jews to Rotterdam port, Dirk and Smit had transported fifteen people (in eight journeys) to various parts of the port, and then onto other fishing vessels that found their way to England. It was only a small boat. But, so far, it had worked just fine, as the old man had a storage section at the bottom of the boat, where two or three people could lie flat.
Smit shivered in the cool breeze, as he turned another street corner. He could hear the echo of footsteps against the cobbled street behind him.
It was the 824th day of German occupation.

Five Days in May

Gary S Smith

CHAPTER EIGHT

ROTTERDAM FROM THE SKY

"Alone and above all else" (Motto for Squadron 541)

30th August 1942, RAF Benson, Oxfordshire, England.

Kobus walked across the runway towards his Spitfire, full of pride and anticipation. He took a deep breath and filled in lungs with fresh morning air. His first solo operational reconnaissance flight awaited him. It's a pity last night's hangover from the White Hart Pub was still making its presence felt as the headache prevailed. Last night had been a heavy night in the pub, because he wasn't scheduled to be flying this morning. Six games of darts, and the same number of pints of British ale. The glasses were bigger in England. "Pint glasses" they called them. Much bigger than the small Dutch glasses used for Dutch beer. It was funny because the English were generally smaller people than the Dutch, but they would drink ale from large glasses …and at great speed as if it was a race. Maybe it was because the ale was at room temperature, and easier to drink faster. It didn't take long for Kobus to work out that the best way to forge relationships with his new colleagues was to go down to the pub. Now it seemed that Kobus, had finally been accepted amongst his peers. Especially as

Five Days in May

they had learned the Dutch word for "cheers !", which was "Prost!". This was said with increased gusto every time a new round of drinks arrived. By the sixth pint the table of pilots (Gordon, Carter, Taylor and Kobus) they were standing up, clinking glasses and shouting "Prost!" to the amusement of the locals.
This morning, part of Kobus's hangover recovery had involved several tea fueled meetings including; - (i) meeting at the met (weather) office, *with a cup of tea* (ii) intelligence briefing, *with two cups of tea (and biscuits)* (iii) a short drive over to the flight offices, to mark out their courses and times, and routes on the maps.....*cup of tea offered but declined (biscuits accepted)*. Spitfires didn't have toilet facilities at 35,000 ft.

The day had started when Flight Lt. Stevenson had asked Kobus into his office to inform him to stand in for another pilot who was too ill to fly.

"Van Hooten, we are in a *bit of pickle*, because Flying Officer Carter has been taken into hospital last night. Today, I want you to do a sortie over Rotterdam," said Stevenson, hardly looking up from desk where he was making his daily target list.

"Yes sir, it is ....home grass for me," said Kobus.
"Ah, you mean, *home turf*," said Stevenson smiling.
"Exactly sir, I'm from Rotterdam," said Kobus.
"Ah yes, I knew you were Dutch," said Stevenson. "I'm dreadfully sorry, but there's not much left of Rotterdam, old chap," said Stevenson in a low apologetic tone.
There was a silent pause, as a mark of respect.
Then suddenly Stevenson, stood up brightly and shook Kobus's hand.
"Good luck Van Hooten and keep your eyes peeled," said Stevenson, with a nod that hinted that the meeting was over, and it was time for Kobus to leave,

Gary S Smith

"Thank you, sir," said Kobus.

Van Hooten had consumed so much information over the last few weeks, his mind was in a spin, and now he started to do his final checks as he walked round the Spitfire.

-CHOCKS IN POSITION – yes
-CLEAVER IS IN COLD AIR – yes
-OIL PRESSURE RELIEF VALVE IS CLOSED – yes

He barely noticed the ground crewman and the camera man, hovering around his plane.
"Good morning. Lovely day for flying," said Kobus as he looked up at the blue sky that was littered was small puffy clouds. "How many exposures are in the magazine?"
"300, sir," said the camera man, who stood with his hands in his pockets looking slightly disinterested.
Kobus thought that 150 pictures over each target was okay. As he climbed into the cockpit, he started to go through his list in his mind;-

-CLOSE HOOD PROPERLY (its minus 30 up there) – *yes*
-MIRRORS IN ONE OR TWO BLISTERS (to enable the pilot to see if he is leaving a trail) – *yes, two.*
-TURN ON CAMERAS – *yes*
-TURN ON OXYGEN TO CHECK ITS WORKING – *yes*
-GLOVES ON – *yes*
-ENGINE STARTED – *yes, oh come on Kobus, that's pretty obvious.*

The Merlin engine roared into life, and Kobus pushed the throttle forwards and the PR Mark IV Spitfire began to taxi along the runway. As it picked up speed, Kobus felt a shiver down his spine. He was going home. *Well, actually, 30,000 feet above his home.*

Five Days in May

-ON THE RUN UP CHECK THE AMMETER - *check*

The Spitfire raced along the runway until the accelerating aircraft reached the climactic moment when the wheels left the ground, and the aircraft rose sharply. He loved that feeling of weightlessness on take- off and it seemed as if he was entering into another world. Once the adrenalin of take-off had subsided, Kobus gradually took his Spitfire up to 25,000 feet, flying southeast over the rural villages of Berkshire, Hampshire and Dorset: towards France. It only took a few minutes to actually cross the channel, as soon as the blanket of blue sea had turned into land, Kobus was flying over Nazi occupied France.

This is where the mission really started. At this moment, Kobus started to look around much more frequently for enemy aircraft. The coastal belt was always dangerous due to the location of German radar stations and the proximity of Luftwaffe bases. But now at 30,000 ft, Kobus felt alone, because he was alone in many respects. There was no navigator to read the map or training instructor or co-pilot to give advice. No radio and no guns for defence. He was a "one man show" and he needed eyes in the back of his head.
So, Kobus started to talk to himself, to repeat the advice of Flight Lt. Stevenson. *Good luck keep your eyes pruned......or was it peeled ?... it was 'peeled' come-on Kobus!, pay attention !.*

Kobus occasionally glanced down at his map to check his route. He immediately looked into the mirror of one of the blisters and saw that he was leaving condensation trails. *Shit! Kobus, what are you doing ?.* He dropped the plane down by 500 feet. Checked his mirror, and the trails were still there. *Still white trails !.* He dropped another 500 ft, at last the trails stopped.
Thank God for that. Hopefully an enemy plane or AAK on the ground hadn't spotted him.

Kobus started to panic, he was making basic errors and knew that the fatality rate of new PR pilots was quite high. He gripped his steering stick tighter. He turned the plane sharply to the left into a cirrus cloud and turned to the right. Visibility was now down to a few hundred metres, and he felt safer and began to hum a Glen Miller tune. *Keep alert Kobus.* Talking to himself was helpful. Five minutes later he came out of the cloud. Blue sky all around. 30,000 ft. Eventually he could see the vast forest of the Ardennes of Belgium, below. *Nearly there.*
Fuel was OK. Looking behind. *No trails, no jumpers. Looking above, below, and behind. All good, so far.*

As Kobus flew over Holland towards Rotterdam, his heart skipped a beat as he recognized the terrain. The flat green fields, canals, dykes, churches and then ….the River Rhine. He began to think of his family. His father would be reading De Telegraaf and smoking his pipe now, in his favourite armchair. His mother would be sewing or baking. Soon he would be flying above his own house.
Kobus knew the Rotterdam area from both on the ground and above, from training flights with the Dutch Airforce, so he didn't need to confirm his route on the map. He knew this area like the back of his hand. He followed the River Rhine that snaked across Rotterdam. He began to activate his cameras as he passed over the targets in the Mallegat and the Cude Plantage. *Easy.* 200 photographs taken. Also, not much cloud cover, so the photographs should be clear. Approximately 100 left for his final target: Coolhaven. The Rhine was probably full of German barges, and ships. Kobus tried to disconnect the emotions of flying over his home town… but then he saw the devastation of the Rotterdam city centre and huge areas of flattened ground, where the city once proudly stood. The middle of the city was now reduced to a level wasteland. Kobus was shocked and couldn't take his eyes off the missing parts of the city that had been erased by bombing.

Five Days in May

Even at 30,000 feet the clarity of the destruction was enough to shock Kobus into a state of despair and disbelief. It was if a giant bulldozer had flattened half of the city centre. Kobus felt the sickness rising in his stomach. *How many of his friends and family had been killed or made homeless?.*
This was the result of the German Junker bomber attack of 14th May 1940. Flight Lt. Stevenson was right, there wasn't much left of the city of Rotterdam. *Civilians. Poor bastards* on the ground *had to suffer from the bombing and then live their lives amongst the ruins.*
Kobus's thoughts were interrupted as he began his turn towards the last target area at Coolhaven, when all hell broke loose. The puffs of flak were pounding the sky all around his Spitfire. After a slight pause of two seconds. Kobus turned sharply to the right to run a straight course over his target. Suddenly the plane was shifted violently sideways by the pounding flak. *Jesus Christ!* hissed Kobus as he gripped the controls whilst the plane shook violently. *That was close.* The flak became more intense. Kobus took some photographs quickly, but then he decided to turn the plane quickly westwards back to England. He was worried about damage to his aircraft. His greatest fear was the plane catching fire and being trapped inside and becoming toasted alive. But for now, he checked his tail – *nothing.* He checked above – *nothing.*
He checked below – *Nothing* ! . Kobus had the feeling that he was still caught in a spider's web that he had to somehow wriggle and fight his way out of. The claustrophobia of the cockpit began to intimidate Kobus. Gradually a wave of fear crept over Kobus increasing the fragility of his mortality. Despite all his training, and constantly looking around for German fighter planes, he realized that his apparent survival of the flak from the anti-aircraft guns, was luck. Pure luck.
Kobus began to pray to God as he increased his acceleration on the throttle and made dog leg turns. At this

altitude Kobus was closer to God now, his rebellious passion for atheism had been left behind on the ground. Left then right. He was burning extra fuel by doing this, *bugger the fuel*. Right now, survival was the best option. Eventually the flak subsided. He nervously hummed Glen Miller tunes again, this time crazily out of tune. Travelling back already seemed longer than his outbound journey. He checked the map and the time. Eventually he was over the cloudier skies of Belgium, and then France as he recognized the port of Dunkirk, he began to feel an optimistic surge of relief.

Just over Dunkirk, Kobus snatched glimpses of the blue channel beneath the broken carpet of white clouds. *Don't get complacent now.* Many pilots were lost because they got spotted first and got jumped by German fighter planes such as the Focke Wulf 190 (Fw 190's). Over the channel he could now see the white cliffs of Dover reflecting in the sun. A beautifully welcoming sight. Suddenly two fighter aircraft appeared flying directly towards Kobus. 700 metres, *Fw190s ? no….500 metres* . Kobus recognized them as the American Lockheed P-38 Lightning's, due to their distinctive twin booms. 300 metres, *Yes, pretty sure, they are P-38 lightnings.*
Next came the dreaded "rat-tat-tat-tat!" of the guns, then louder "RAT-TAT-TAT-TAT!!". They were firing *at him!*. *Friendly fire.*
Stupid bastards!.
Kobus turned sharply to the left and dived violently 1,000 feet. They were both on his tail, and Kobus took a gamble and began to climb and turned the Spitfire in a steep turn to show them the plan shape of the Spitfire. They immediately got the message, waggled their wings and zoomed past, and made a turn to back into their original direction.
Thank God, for that.
The rest of the journey was thankfully uneventful as he

flew over the home counties to reach the RAF base in sunny Oxfordshire. Kobus was buzzing with excitement as he touched down at RAF Benson. As soon as he climbed out of the cockpit and got down from the Spitfire and he walked over to the intelligence office, with a sense of pride, to hand cannister of films over the intelligence office. Job done. Kobus had no idea what the photographs (that he had risked his life for) would lead to, as few people in the theatre of war had knowledge of 'the full picture'. Hopefully some German barges, and ammunition factories could be destroyed. Mission complete. Now he felt like a real pilot.

He walked into the mess room with bounce in his stride, enjoying the sensation of having his feet on the ground. Kobus made a cup of tea and walked over to a table where other pilots who had just returned from their missions, were swapping stories. Porter pulled out a chair for Kobus to sit down. He was *one of them* now, but he did not want to show excitement or fear, in the atmosphere of self-controlled calmness. Kobus used both hands to lift up his cup of tea. He didn't want the others to see his shaking hand.

Tonight, it would probably be six or seven pints of ale, but he would give the darts a miss. This time he had stories to tell his colleagues, rather than just listening to the stories of other operational sorties. A shaky hand is not compatible with successful darts play.

Gary S Smith

CHAPTER NINE

RESISTANCE

10th September 1942, Rotterdam

Dirk was killing time in the Café Rouge holding the front page of De Telegraaf. There was a large photograph of the Mayor of Amsterdam (a member of the Dutch NSB) shaking hands with a German General. Both were smiling, like old friends. "Propaganda," muttered Dirk as he sniffed in a cynical gesture and took a sip of his coffee. He managed to miss his mouth and the coffee dripped over the newspaper, blotting the exchange rate between the German Mark and the Dutch Guilder. He would have to listen to Radio Oranje or the BBC, later on, for reliable news.

Dirk was waiting for Smit and two other members of the resistance, George and Frans. The meetings were short and business like. They trusted each other but didn't really get to know each other. If they were caught by the Gestapo and tortured – the less they knew about their accomplices (and resistance activities), then the less chance of their comrades being caught.

Gert, the café owner shuffled over to the table. Gert was an old man, at least seventy and almost completely bald, apart from some short grey hair at the back of his round head, just above his collar. Gert was medium height but his body shape very round, like a football. His expanding waistline was a mystery because his cooking at the café was really terrible. His protruding pot belly placed additional strain on his tightly fitted white apron. It was a quiet day so far in the café with only two customers, which consisted of Dirk, plus an old man seated on a separate table who had been nursing an empty cup of coffee for the last one hour. That was an impressive achievement, sitting on hard wooden chairs in a dark, dingy café for one hour.

The café doorbell rang as Smit, George and Frans entered. They nodded and sat down at Dirk's round table. The normal pleasantries were exchanged, and they began to talk about the Feyenoord football team's latest defeat. As soon as an old man in the corner had left the café, they had the entire café to themselves, apart from Gert who has half deaf. The topic of conversation changed.

Smit opened his new packet of Dutch cigarettes and extended four cigarettes from the packet to offer them around. The three were quickly snapped up.
They lit up their cigarettes and leaned back in their chairs exhaling the smoke to form a big cloud that quickly filled the small cafe. The café owner wobbled over to the table with four cups of coffee on his tray. He placed each cup on the table, but it looked like the usual average quality coffee, with the usual excuses.
"Sorry gentlemen. The coffee shipments from the colonies have been stopped since 1940, since the Germans took over the docks. So, I'm afraid, it's not the best coffee." Gert bowed his head in remorse and waited for a reaction.

"But for us, there are not many café's left after the bombing, so *beggars can't be choosers*. As long as it's wet and its warm," said Dirk "it will do."
Gert was quite deaf, so he took this as compliment from

another satisfied customer.

"Can I get some food for you, gentlemen?" said Gert.

"No!" said Dirk, "I'm fine," holding his hand up, just to be absolutely clear.

"No!!" the others chimed in unison, Smit holding up both hands (ready to push back the food). It seemed even Frans and George knew about the poor food.

"That's a pity, because I have some lovely Erwetensoep on the stove," said Gert. He hobbled away with the empty tray clutched to his chest.

The four resumed their conversation.

"Anymore fishing trips being planned?" said Dirk.

Frans and George nodded politely. They both looked nervous. Frans was fidgeting with his shirt, and George was stroking his mustache. They were ready to propose a new plan to Dirk (expanding the smuggling operation).

"Gents, we might be able to get a bigger boat, it can take more fish," said Smit.

"Yes, but we cannot go down the River Maas near the city, the only safe pick up is at the docks not far from the coast," said Frans. He had stopped fidgeting now and seemed serious.

"No. Now is not the time to expand our fishing mission, a bigger boat attracts attention. Unwelcome attention. Sorry Smit the time is not right," said Dirk.

Smit just sucked his teeth and grinned in disappointment. Once again Smit's plan had been openly rejected by Dirk.

The conversation immediately stopped when two German officers walked into the Café. They nodded a greeting as they sat down on a nearby table on the dark wooden seats. The café was quiet now, you could hear a pin drop. Smit leaned back on his chair, running his hand through his thin blonde hair and spoke in German.

"Excuse me, sir, I can recommend the food here, it is the best traditional Dutch food in Rotterdam," said Smit.

Gary S Smith

"Danker," said the German officer who did not appear convinced, but seemed relieved that they had been made welcome. He opened up his German newspaper and took out his packet German cigarettes (Neu Front).
Gert shuffled over to the German table as fast as possible. Eyes widened at the prospect of selling some food.

After the invasion, during the five days of May 1940, the Germans tried to be friendly with the Dutch. The Germans saw the Dutch as *almost* equals, as they were part of the Germanic race. At first, the Germans tried to show friendliness towards the Dutch people. These offerings were ungraciously received as the Netherlands was a proud and independent nation who had successfully fought off previous foreign invaders (including Spain and France). The Germans were placed in the same category. They were foreign invaders; it was a simple as that.

Slowly as the occupation period evolved, the changes in Dutch life became apparent. Newspapers were closed down, one by one. Dutch people caught listening to Radio Oranje or the BBC were imprisoned. Rationing becoming harsher, as coffee, rice, sugar, tea and chocolate became scarce. In nearly all Dutch towns, Nazi uniforms were everywhere, especially at railway stations as deterrence against sabotage. The prohibitions began to increase over the five year occupation period. The mayors of most towns were replaced by Dutch Nazi members (NSB). The boy scout movement was abolished on the basis that the boy scout movement was associated with its British origins.

Dirk finished the last of his coffee and stubbed out his cigarette in this white porcelain ash tray and tilted his head towards the café door. It was a signal to leave. They started to move tentatively towards the door, trying but failing to make their exit look natural.

Dirk pulled the door handle downwards to open the café door. He stopped in his tracks.

"Papers please, gentlemen," said the more senior German officer.

The four men turned around one hundred and eighty degrees and began to produce their papers and place them on the table. One by one. The older German officer looked at them quickly, apart from Smit's papers which he perused with great care.

"Wilhelm Smit hhhmmm …a good German name," said the German officer smiling sarcastically. He paused, while he looked at Smit's face waiting for a reaction that did not come. "Ahh. Former soldier in the Dutch army. A short career that lasted for ….five days."
Both German officers threw back their heads and laughed. The booming laughter seemed to go on for some time. The four dutchmen didn't laugh. They stood, heads down and stared at Gert's dusty wooden floor.
"…and now working at the railway station. Good boy Smit. I just hope your recommendation of *traditional* food, is good, and not some kind of joke."
He handed the paper back to the Dutchmen.
Smit touched his cap in salute "It depends on your tolerance of foreign food."
"Goedenmiddag" said Dirk as a signal to accelerate their departure from the café. Dirk nudged Smit in the back, as Dirk was shuffling his paper back into his coat pocket.
"Good day gentlemen," said the German officer in German without looking up from his fake coffee.

The four men left the café without further ado. The four men began to walk away quickly. Dirk had been irritated by Smit's behaviour in the café, but he waited until the café was out of sight.

Dirk stood in front of Smit, blocking his path. "What *are* you playing at?"
"I'm Just being polite to the foreign occupying force," said Smit light heartedly.
"This is no joke, Smit. You're drawing attention to you AND US !. We don't need attention."
There was a pause. Frans and George were in silent agreement.

"You all know, what happens to us, if we get caught by the Germans for helping Jews to escape…"
"..and remember our families would be tortured and killed," said Frans. George nodded in agreement.
"This is dangerous business, which is why most civilians won't take the risk of getting involved in the resistance," said George, who had only really spoken now for the first time.
There was another pause.
"Please have a long think about the risk involved in providing your boat and getting more involved. Especially your families," said Dirk. The four men had stopped walking now.
Frans nodded silently. George's facial expression was hidden by his large mustache, which he stroked with his finger.
They began walking along the pavement again, two by two. The street was quiet. Smit was walking next to Dirk, hand in pockets but his eyes were fixed downwards as if he had been scolded. Each man was deep in his own thoughts. Torn between a sense of duty and self-preservation.
"I guess, we need a new café to meet at," said Dirk.
"The coffee was only average anyway," said Frans trying to lighten the mood.
"…and the food was disgusting," said Dirk.

"The bread was like sawdust and the cheese was like shoe leather," said Smit.
They continued to walk down the street. The unmistakable bald headed figure of Van De Raal was walking towards them with confident long strides. His long trench coat ballooned like a parachute against the oncoming breeze.
"Morning gentlemen. Going anywhere nice?"
"Walking around in our God given ways," said Dirk nodding his head continuing his walk.
Nobody spoke until they were a safe distance from De Rat.
"Verrada," said Smit.
"These days. De Rat is sniffing around everywhere," said George.
"I can't wait to shoot that bastard," said Dirk.
"It's a waste of bullet, we should use Rat poison instead !" said George.
The four men laughed discretely.
"Smit, you're a good scout," said Dirk as he patted Smit on the back. Smit felt some emotional warmth from the gesture, but somehow patronized. He was twenty three years old now, and Smit considered that he was now worthy of being treated like a man.

When they reached the crossroads the four men wordlessly went their separate ways.
At the crossroads a mother and a teenage child were turning into the road which housed the Café rouge. The twelve year old was dribbling a brown leather football on the wet pavement. The mother was carrying a shopping bag. It seemed like a completely normal scene, except both were wearing a yellow arm band showing the Star of David.

Gary S Smith

CHAPTER TEN

THE KNOCK

11th September 1942, Rotterdam

Smit had been staying at his parents' house in the city, since they had left in the summer of 1940 to live with relatives in a village near Breda (south Holland). They believed it was safer in the village: Less Nazis and more food. Since then, Smit had the house to himself and he had enjoyed the independence.

This had suited Smit, as he had set up his own Bachelor pad where he had his own radio, leather sofa, log fireplace, and good stock of wine and whiskey. So far he had not been successful in bringing a woman back to his house because Smit was usually too drunk to be a successful Casanova. So, he spent many evenings in the house listening to the radio, or reading the Trouw newspaper, under the flickering candlelight. He also used the house for resistance meetings.

Early morning around 6.00 a.m. Smit heard a knock at the door. It was not a quiet or polite knock. It was a loud banging on the door. A knock screaming of urgency.

Smit pulled his trousers on and grabbed a shirt that was loosely hanging over a chair near his bed. As he rubbed his eyes to wake up, the banging on the door continued. This time louder. Smit was anxious, *this could only mean one thing*.

As he unlocked the door and gripped the handle, the door flew open banging into Smit's face. Stunned and on the

back foot he stumbled backwards. A man in a black Gestapo uniform punched Smit who fell on the lounge floor. When Smit looked up the Gestapo man was pointing a pistol at Smit's head. "Wilhelm Smit ?"
"Yes," said Smit in a barely audible whisper.
"Hand hoch!" he screamed. Three or four German soldiers with Schmeisser guns walked quickly into the house. They started to search the rooms with reckless violence. One by one with a brutally efficient methodology.
"Anybody else, staying here with you in the house?" said the Gestapo officer.
"No, just me," said Smith, who was conscious that he still had his hands raised high in a surrender position.
Smit was disturbed by the scene unfolding before his sleepy eyes and tried to restore some composure.
"Why are you here?, what have I done?"
"Good questions. Soon we will have *all* the answers. Sit down, over there," said the Gestapo man. Although he looked middle aged with his distinctive round, steel rimmed glasses, he was probably only mid-thirties in age. His flat officer hat was tilted over his forehead, but it could not hide his short and stocky build. Behind him stood a Dutch NSB traitor, wearing a brown Nazi uniform. Smit recognized him from school. Nils and Smit had been friends on the same hockey team.
As the German jack boots trampled around the wooden floor, moving furniture, emptying drawers, removing paintings from the wall and then throwing them onto the floor. Smit focused on Nils who appeared to be guarding the front door and spoke in Dutch quickly with a heavy Rotterdam dialect to the Dutch Nazi.
"Aaah, Nils?, is that you hiding in the NSB Nazi uniform?"
Nils nodded proudly.
"What exactly are you looking for? your rotten conscience ? said Smit as he leaned back in his chair, pretending to

Five Days in May

look confident.

Nils could not look at Smit directly in the eye. He looked at the fireplace and spoke in an official tone. "We are here to search your house as there are reports of suspicious activity....Wilhelm Smit."

"That's nonsense. What happened to you Nils? Waking up innocent people at 0600 and smashing up people's houses....you're making a real contribution to the Rotterdam community..."

Nils walked towards Smit, stood straight, trying to restrain himself.

"The terrorist resistance does not help the Rotterdam community. Quite the opposite. Now if you tell us about your resistance work and give us *names*, we'll stop the search."

The German soldiers moved the lounge rug to the side of the room and began to spring open the floorboards with a crowbar.

Smit continued to speak quickly in Dutch, again applying a strong Rotterdam dialect so that the Germans would not understand

"Do you remember the bombings of 14th May 1940?. How did this destruction help the community?"

"You know that was an accident, *caused* by the Dutch government's stupid refusal to surrender. Be careful Smit. Your mouth is quicker than your brain," said Nils. He had a point.

"This *Swein* will talk soon. Enough of this!" said the Gestapo man clenched the Luger pistol by the barrel end and swung his arm at Smit. Smit felt a crushing blow to the back of his head and Smit saw stars, blackness and then nothing. The curtains in the house were drawn.

****

Gary S Smith

The next day, Smit woke up on a cold hard floor. He had a dull throbbing headache. It wasn't a hangover. He carefully massaged a large bruise on the back of his head. Then he rubbed the stubble on his chin and began to recollect his thoughts as he wondered where he was and how he got there. His house had been searched and somebody had knocked him out. Smit started to look around at his prison cell. Maybe eight feet by Sixteen feet. There was a heavy wooden door, battleship grey. The walls were even darker, in charcoal black. There was a cold dampness in the room, with condensation on the walls. The only furniture was an old bed on the back wall. Above the bed was a small window which was blacked out. He felt thirsty and hungry. His mother had always said it wasn't healthy to miss out on breakfast.
He sat up, cross legged and realised that all he had was his shoes, trousers and a shirt still half buttoned up. Smit ran his grubby hands through his fine blonde hair and waited.

Smit wondered if the Gestapo had actually found anything in the house search. There was an underground newspaper called "Het Parool" that Smit had kept under his mattress, and radio in the laundry room. All of that was *passive resistance* and illegal, but not unusual. Smit was more worried about the guns buried in the back garden. The publication Het Parool was very popular and the circulation had increased as the German treatment of the Dutch became gradually harsher, the Dutch resistance became stronger. Smit knew that smuggling Jews known as Onkerduikers ("underdivers") from Holland to England was an activity punishable by death. Smit's involvement in the resistance had bought Smit a ticket into a prison cell. *A one way ticket ?*

Think Smit, think ! what else could they find?. Smit had almost forgotten about the maps of England, Belgium and France, the foreign currency, and a small collection of knives. They were under the floor boards in his bedroom.

Three days in complete isolation passed by and the same thoughts circled around Smits head. The resistance, the pending examination, and his fragile mortality. Smit was twenty-three years old. So far, he had only had two girlfriends, and there could have been more. He didn't want to drag a girl into the resistance with the associated dangers. Dirk had told him that the resistance was for loners, who had to act and think alone; and to say nothing. Smit had always struggled with that last bit. In his short life he had only travelled to Belgium and Germany, but he had not yet "Travelled the world". All things considered, Smit had not experienced much life at all. He might never get the chance to find a life-partner, get married or start a family. This was the tragic consequence of dying young. Smit held his head in his hands and rubbed his forehead, searching for an answer: a way out of this situation. Smit had been warned by his friends of the dangers of joining the resistance. That is why many did not join and put their lives (and their family's lives) on the line. He could understand that now.

These thoughts continuously circulated around Smit's brain. Each day the NSB guard brought in a lump of bread and a cup of water and asked him in Dutch if Smit was ready to speak to the Germans. Smit shook his head, each time. Smit was buying extra time for Dirk and his comrades. So far, three days and counting. Next to Smit's bed, somebody had scratched three letters on to the wall "OZO" (meaning "Orange Will Win"). Smit shivered and folded his arms to keep warm. He wondered if the person who scratched this graffiti had lived or died.

Gary S Smith

CHAPTER ELEVEN

TOT ZIENS

14th September 1940, Rotterdam.

Dirk sat on the bench watching the early morning mist drift across the River Rhine. The hypnotic scene increased his sense of melancholia. Since Smit had been taken in by the local NSB and Gestapo, Dirk had been anxiously waiting for news. Waiting for news was helplessly agonizing, especially when the news was most likely to be bad news. He was constantly moving around like a cat on a hot tin roof. For Dirk it felt like the beginning of the end of his small resistance group. His choice was either to run – and leave Rotterdam - or to stay and carry on as normal and keep a low profile. The last option would only work if Smit kept his mouth shut and didn't give the names of his resistance comrades to the Gestapo. Smit was a nice lad, but he had a big mouth.

It was very quiet. There was nobody else next to the River at 0730, only the odd fishing boat, or the occasional old man taking his dog for a walk on the path that followed the river. There was a nip in the air and Dirk turned up his coat collar and then looked at his watch, 0735: George was late. Luckily they both worked at the Railway station, so they could walk there together and catch up on the news about Smit.

Dirk heard a coughing noise behind him, and he swung his head round quickly, giving him a crick in the neck. He saw George's shadowy figure approaching through the fog. George had a big frame, a big mustache, round face, and straight brown hair touching his collar. His hair was a little longer than the fashionable short back and sides. Dirk thought that George looked like a bear.

"Hallo, you scared me," said Dirk standing up rubbing his neck.

"Hoi," said George smiling

"Let's walk and talk," said Dirk.

"I have news about Smit," said George as they started to walk slowly.

"Go on, tell me," said Dirk, searching for his cigarettes. Since Smit had been taken in by the Gestapo Dirk had been chain smoking and not sleeping much.

George flipped open his cigarette packet pulling out two cigarettes, and both men stopped and lit up.

"I found out some information from my contact : he's alive, but they are holding him as a prisoner in the cells in the Gestapo headquarters, Rotterdam," said George.

"I thought so. But he has been there for three days now," said Dirk.

"Yes. Poor bastard. I hope he is okay. Let's hope he doesn't talk and give names," said George exhaling the smoke through his nose.

"It's too risky to rely on hope, they will be torturing him. He's just a young lad. They'll be threatening his family. So, it's only a matter of time. You know that most prisoners don't leave that building alive?" said Dirk.

"Yeah, and the ones that leave are usually sent to the camps," nodded George.

Dirk lowered his voice as they left the river path and headed towards a nearby street. Only a ten minute walk from the station.

"The Germans will be *all over* our houses, and those *slimy*

Five Days in May

NSB bastards will be sniffing around and informing on us. They are everywhere, like rats!" said Dirk.

"George. Remind Frans. Nothing suspicious. Keep your houses clean, relocate any weapons or evidence."

"Schoon," confirmed George. He was a man of few words, but solid and trustworthy.

"George. Do me one favour. Send a letter to Dirk's family advising them to leave their homes immediately and go to live somewhere in complete secret. The Gestapo will be planning to imprison or assassinate members of Smit's family to make Smit talk." Dirk handed George an envelope with the names and addresses of Smit's family.

"No problem. I will send the anonymous letters today," said George.

A man walked passed them on the opposite side of the road, and Dirk felt exposed. Eyes were everywhere.

"Now, when we get to the end of the street I will stop off at the shop, but you carry on walking. We cannot be seen together" said Dirk.

"George. Remind our own people. No activities until all of this investigation has blown over. Anything to do with the resistance. No radios, no underground newspapers, and especially no hiding places for Dutch Jews," said Dirk.

"No more Onkerduikers (underdivers) now. It's too dangerous, they will search all of our houses. Top to Bottom," said George.

"Listen Dirk, the game is up. Me and Frans will go on the run and hide somewhere for a few months until all of this interrogation business has finished."

There was a slight pause while both men were thinking of the measures that would have to be taken, to sweep over their tracks.

"Hey Dirk? ....are you afraid ?" said George.

"Yes. I can't sleep. And *you* should be afraid as well."

They walked together in silence. George stopped and turned to Dirk. "I guess this is it then ?"

Gary S Smith

"Yes, it is. George, if anything happens to Smit we must inform our fellow resistance people that De Rat is a suspected informer?. Dirk handed George another envelope wrapped in a handkerchief. George nodded and grinned.
They both knew that this was goodbye
"Hey Dirk, OZO (Orange will win)" said George.
"Tot Ziens," (meaning "see you later") said Dirk as he shook hands with George firmly and immediately turned to walk down the road, alone.

Dirk was due to start his shift at the railway station at 9.00 a.m. He fumbled around in his coat pocket for his cigarettes. He realized he had finished his last one an hour ago. With so much on his mind he had forgotten to buy a new packet.

Five Days in May

Gary S Smith

CHAPTER TWELVE

A QUESTION OF TIME

"I felt peace, even though I was still scared to death. I thought that, whatever would happen to me - I could still be killed. I didn't know - and in what I'd already been through, God was in control."
[— Diet Eman, Things We Couldn't Say]

15th September 1942, Rotterdam.

On the fourth day Smit heard the echo of footsteps outside his prison cell. The keys rattled in the lock and the thick wooden door was opened. The short, fat NSB guard walked into the room with a sense of purpose, and a ridiculous air of authority. He looked at Smit, blankly, and said "At 2.00 a.m. you will be examined." He turned on his heal and walked straight out of the room, with the door slamming behind him, for good effect.
The brief visit had revived Smit's dulled senses. Smit paced up and down the cell. Again, he lay on the bed. Paced up and down the cell and repeated this process countless times. This was pure nervous energy as a result of being

confined to a small space but having to deal with the mind games being played by his captors. He was thinking of staying strong but wondered if he would break under torture. He did some press ups to relieve the tension and then lay on the bed. Smit stayed awake, reasserting his strategy of maintaining silence throughout interrogation.

At around 2.00 a.m. the noise of keys jangling alerted Smit who immediately sat up straight in anticipation for the dreaded "examination".

The door opened, and the short fat NSB guard took two paces into the room and announced, "The Interview is cancelled."

"Sweet dreams," said the guard just before the door slammed. The noise reverberated inside Smit. The prolonged echo was haunting. Smit had mixed feelings about the postponement, he did not know whether to feel relived or disappointed. However, Smit knew that inevitably it would take a good interview performance by Smit to secure his release from prison.

The light switch had been turned on outside the room, and Smit could not switch it off as there was no light switch on the inside of his cell. Smit began to suspect that the permanent light and the interview postponements was all part of a game. Smit tried to relax in vain, desperately in search of peaceful sleep. He tried to shelter from reality by dipping into his daydreams of yesterdays.

The same thing happened the next day. The 2.00 a.m. interview was arranged and cancelled; and the next day. Smit knew what was happening. Smit had heard that sleep deprivation was mental torture, and Smit was beginning to experience this, first hand. The lack of food and water made him feel weak. Smit was talking to himself. "*Grind it out*" he thought. He clenched his fist in anger. Anger against the Germans, anger against the NSB, but mostly, his anger was directed against himself as Smit had not been

careful enough. Despite warnings from the likes of Dirk. He cursed at his public display of arrogance against the Germans in the café, his many meetings in public in the same places, with small groups of locals. His indiscreet distribution of the underground newspaper on the streets. He cursed at his over enthusiastic recruitment campaign for new members of the resistance. His anger towards the informer was a slow burning anger that would never subside. He would take revenge. The informer was most likely De Rat, and Smit began to think of the different ways to kill him. *Knife or gun ? probably knife. That would be slower.*
The problem in Smit's mind was that the informer could have been anybody from a network of around twenty people. Smit had been "*too* active," and careless.
As the days passed by, Smit was plagued by self-doubt, and he became physically and mentally weaker.

On day seven it started. The short fat guard opened the cell room door and he was followed by two Gestapo officers', both wearing long black leather coats. They all stood and stared at Smit, sizing him up. Smit sat on his bed, trying to look relaxed, but fidgeted by rubbing his eyes and his cheeks with the palm of both hands. They were weighing him up. Yes, he was a mess. Smit was ripe for questioning.
"Any chance of a cigarette ?" said Smit.

There was a silent pause. Smit regretted the flippant question.

Smit had chance now to study the two Gestapo officers, who had initially looked the same, but now after closer scrutiny seemed rather different, as there were human beings living behind the facade of the uniform. The older officer showed some signs of grey hair underneath his black Gestapo hat, which contrasted with his black shirt,

black trousers, and black leather coat. He was like an undertaker. His belly protruded over his leather belt. The local food shortages had clearly not affected the Gestapo.
His partner wore the same clothes but was slimmer and younger. He wore spectacles, but that did not shield his piercing eyes, and sadistic grin.
"That depends on if you talk….or if you don't talk Mr. Smit." The grey haired Gestapo man said moving his head sideways to beckon Smit out of the cell.
Smit was hand-cuffed and was marched down the corridor. His legs were stiff, but his heart beat raced as he was finally led out of his tiny damp, dark cell that had been his home for nearly a week.

Along the corridor, they stopped outside a room, where the door was wide open. Smit craned his neck to look inside. It was a large room, with hooks hanging from the middle of the ceiling. There was one man hanging upside down and his body was littered with scars and bruises; Smit noticed that there were speckles of blood on the floor. The man's noise was caked in dried blood, but although Smit studied the gruesome spectacle, but he still could not tell if the poor bastard was dead or just unconscious.

The scary Gestapo man with the spectacles turned around and said to Smit.
"That's what happens when you DON'T talk."
Smit just stared back at the body, expressionless, trying not to betray the simmering fear inside him.

Smit was led further down the corridor, into another room. As the heavy wooden door opened the brightness of the room was dazzling Smit, who blinked fiercely. Smit cautiously walked into the room, his legs still felt stiff. The walls had been freshly painted white and there were two powerful light bulbs. It took a long time to adjust. He sat

down on a wooden chair at a table facing the two Gestapo men.
"Tell me Smit, are you a member of the Resistance?"
Smit just rubbed his eyes and said nothing.
"We found a radio in your house. What did you listen to? BBC or radio Orange ?"
"German music. *Wagner*," said Smit.
"You were a member of the Dutch army, Smit ?" said the grey Gestapo man, who spoke like a kindly doctor.
"Yes, I fought for my country, is that a crime?" said Smit.
While Smit was looking at the doctor, Smit felt a punch hit him square on the nose. Smit's head recoiled backwards. Smit was shocked as he hadn't seen the punch coming and now he felt the stinging pain. He rubbed his nose. No blood. The punch had come from the scary one with the spectacles.
"Mr. Smit. You have been seen conspiring and plotting with groups of men in the city," said the doctor calmly.
Smit shrugged his shoulders.
"I am allowed to talk to people. I have friends," said Smit quietly.
"We found a resistance newspaper in your house," said the doctor.
Suddenly the doctor stood up, raised his hand and banged his fist down on the table. The bang echoed around the windowless room. Smit jumped up in his chair. It was natural reaction. His nerves were on edge. He was now expecting another punch. The embarrassment of his fear increased his fragility.

"Tell us about the boat, you use to smuggle the Jews from Rotterdam to England."

Smit said nothing. There was a pause of a couple of minutes. The doctor banged his fist on the table, again. Smit was surprised by how loud it seemed, it made his nerves jangle uncontrollably. Smit was disturbed that he could not control his physical reactions.

"Gives us the names of the other resistance terrorist!" screamed the scary man. His face contorted with rage.
Smit said nothing and stared at the wall.
The next punch caught Smit on the cheekbone, followed by another on the chin. Smit could taste the blood in his mouth from his busted lip. Smit felt dizzy and nauseous.
There was another pause, which may have been for a few minutes, but it seemed like hours.
"We know you have …..*family*.." said the doctor.
The two men looked at each other and then left the room and slammed the door. He heard the key turn in the lock and Smit breathed a sigh of relief. Smit looked at his watch. He had only been in that room for forty-five minutes, but it had seemed much longer. Now Smit just stared at the white wall and waited. And Waited. Time passed, and Smit lay his head on the table and momentarily for a few minutes drifted off searching for any pleasant memory of the past, but only to return to his gut wrenching present day nightmare.

Suddenly the door crashed open. The two Gestapo men came running into the room. The young scary officer with the glasses launched a kick that knocked Smit backwards whilst still sitting in the chair. Smit had no time to move and the back of his head crashed against the stone floor. Smit was dazed and saw stars.
"Ahhh!" groaned Smit, as he rolled off the chair sideways onto the floor. The two bastards were shouting and screaming at Smit as he curled up on the floor in a fetal position.
"Are you ready to talk !" shouted the doctor.
At the same time the young scary man launched another kick, this time into Smit's groin. Smit tried to cry out, but he was in so much pain that he could only quietly whisper.
"Oh God."

"Names! Now!" screamed the scary one.
"I gave you a name," mumbled Smit, barely audible,
"What name!" shouted the doctor.
"God," said Smit as he curled up into a ball, placing his hands over his head for protection. "....he has just joined the resistance..."
Smit felt multiple kicks to his head and back. Maybe five or six. He was praying for this to be over. One kick landed into his shoulder blade, causing excruciating pain. He wretched and tried to vomit.
The doctor picked Smit up from the floor in a bear hug, dragged him over the table like a rag doll. Smit was tall but skinny. The scary one propped up the chair which was still on its side. The doctor dropped him back into the chair.
Everybody was now sat at the table, quietly. It seemed that everyone was catching their breath back.
"Get the hammer," said the doctor, and the scary one flashed a sly grin towards Smit before he left the room eagerly.
"I warn you Smit, my colleague enjoys using a hammer on his enemies. Better to talk now. Just give me names," said the doctor, in his smooth silky tones.
Smit ran his hand slowly through his hair like a comb, his finger nails gripped on to his scalp. He rocked backwards and forwards still feeling the pain from the kicking. He felt like a child in the playground, seeking refuge from dangerous bullies.
The scary one came back into the room still grinning like an eager child about to play his favourite game. He carefully placed the hammer onto the table.
"Are you left or right handed ?" said the scary one.
"I'm left handed," lied Smit.
The first whack of the hammer banged the table. A purposeful miss, for effect. Although, Smit still felt the anticipated pain.
"I want the names of the terrorist you are working with !"
Smit was dazed with pain and fear but stayed quiet.

Five Days in May

"Both hands spread on the table. Now!"
Smit spread both hands on the table and looked up at the ceiling, to avoid the sight of the hammer smashing into his fingers. An endless pause was followed by a dull crunching noise of Smit's left hand, middle finger. An instant screaming pain shot through from his knuckle. The pain became a dull throb. Smit placed his injured hand under his right armpit.
He looked at the doctor who wore the same expression of a serious doctor curing an ill patient, and then he looked at the scary one. His spectacles seemed to have steamed up with the excitement, but his smile penetrated the Smit's soul. *How could he enjoy torturing civilians? What kind of animal was he?*
Smit said nothing and stared above the heads of his two tormentors at the white wall.
Smit was breathing heavily, and his body was shaking in traumatic shock. It was an unchartered level of pain never experienced before.
Another period of silence.
"I can't give names. Because I don't have any names," said Smit staring at the doctor, trying to look sincere (It was better than staring at the scary one).
The scary one stood up and brought down the hammer from a greater height this time. Smit tensed his body and froze in anticipation. The dull thud of the hammer head smashed mid-way on his second finger. "Aaahhhhhhh!" Smit screamed as the bolt of pain shot through him. The muscles in his body quivered, as he tried to deal with the unbearable agony. Smit now realized that his screaming seemed to help deal with the pain. He was initially disappointed about his screaming reaction, as he wanted to his resilience to remain unbroken. Now the flood gates had opened, and he was no longer in control. The pulsating drum beat of pain was taking over. This torture was effective. It was only a question of time now.

Gary S Smith

The two torturers left the room as Smit looked down at his bloody and broken fingers.
Smit looked at his watch. So far, he has lasted for 2 hours. *How much longer could he last ?*
The doctor came in and placed a pen and paper on the table. He gave a summary of the situation.
"Mr. Smit, we know about you and the resistance, we know about the boat, smuggling Jews to England. We want the names of your collaborators. If we do not have the names in twenty-four hours then your family members will be sent to the camps." The Gestapo officer delivered this statement in calm, clinical way. Like a doctor explaining a prescription for some medicine to cure a disease.
"Write the names on this paper and you are free to go. Otherwise. Tomorrow we start at 0700 and my colleague will start this process again…but this time on your toes."

As he walked towards the door, he stopped.
"Oh, by the way. Earlier, you asked for a cigarette. Have this before you go back to your cell." The doctor lit up a cigarette and offered it to Smit: good medicine from the kind doctor.
Smit struggled to hold the cigarette in his shaking right hand, as he jostled the cigarette in between two fingers he almost dropped it on the floor. Finally he brought the cigarette to his swollen lips and inhaled deeply. The first drag was always the best. He exhaled the smoke through his broken nose, but the smoke stung his bloody mouth. This was Smit's first cigarette in seven days. The doctor stood waiting to see Smit's reaction. The first 'hit' of tobacco made Smit feel dizzy but relaxed. On the second drag Smit swallowed the smoke into his lungs and tasted a combination of blood and tobacco. He became light headed and then nauseous.
"Is it …..Dutch?" said Smit looking at the cigarette.

Five Days in May

"No. Its German. It's called *Neue Front"* ('New Front') The doctor said proudly.
Smit felt the bile rising from his stomach, burning his throat as he doubled up to vomit over the floor. As he wiped the trickles of vomit from his mouth and sat upright he noticed that speckles of vomit had left orange marks across the white wall.
The kind doctor looked disgusted, but resigned to the fact that he had literally extracted the maximum amount from this interrogation session.
"OZO," said Smit, muttering to himself, as he stubbed out the German cigarette into the ashtray.

Gary S Smith

Five Days in May

CHAPTER THIRTEEN

HEROIC BETRAYAL

19th September 1942, Rotterdam

Smit had lasted eight days in the Gestapo headquarters in Rotterdam. He lay on his bed wondering how many more days or hours of torture he could last out.
Any thoughts, of any kind, were interrupted by the constant throbbing pain of his injuries. His broken nose, and bruised jaw were sore, but the kick into his shoulder blades had made it impossible to sleep on his back. He could not sleep on his front due to the broken ribs from the kicking. The two broken fingers were a painful irritation, like major toothache in his fingers.
Needless to say, there hadn't been much sleep. The prison had become noisier over the last couple of days, especially by the screaming noises coming from next door. At around 3.00 am he heard the door of his neighbouring cell open. It was so loud that at first he thought it was Smit's door. Then there was a rush of boots and some scuffling noises of the prisoner being heavily assaulted by a two or maybe three people. It had lasted for five minutes and when his attackers had left, Smit could hear the low moaning noise of his neighbour recovering from his beating. Smit was surprised how the grim sound of whimpering and weeping haunted him so much.

At around 7.00 a.m. the door opened, and the short fat guard walked into the room with his usual air of self-imposed authority. He was in his thirties and his hairline was already receding. "Goedenmiddag," said the short man just before the door slammed.
"Do you have the names?"
"Yes. But I won't give them to a Dutch traitor, a fake Nazi. I will give them to a real German Nazi," said Smit, lethargically. His ribs beginning to hurt again.
The short fat man, advanced two steps towards Smit. Smit flinched, expecting violence.
"Wees Voorzichtig Smit, *if* you leave this building, *if* you leave, you will then need all the friends you can get because you are a traitor to our Furher and you will *also* be a traitor to the resistance," said the short fat man as he picked up the sheet of paper on the floor and handed it carefully to Smit.
"Maybe. Unfortunately, when the Germans have been defeated you will be left all alone, to rot in hell."
Smit clutched the piece of paper in his hands, tucked it inside his blood stained shirt.
"The Third Reich will last for a thousand years, so you'd better get used to it, " said the short fat man, in a matter of fact kind of way.
The short fat man stared at Smit and gave a mischievous smile and walked towards the door and spoke.
"Veal plezier."
"Verrada," said Smit as the door closed.
Smit looked at the piece of paper it was still blank.
For the next three hours nothing happened, and Smit drifted in and out of sleep whilst sitting cross-legged on his bed.
Suddenly, Smit heard the sound of the keys rattled in the door, and the door opened abruptly.
The short fat NSB officer walked in followed by the two Gestapo men. There was an urgency in their movements.

Five Days in May

"You were ordered to write the names on the paper. Give me the names Smit?"
"There are no names. Do you want me to *make up* the names?"
The scary one, took out his luger and marched over the Smit who was still sitting on his bed, staring at the wall. He placed the pistol against Smit's head slowly. Smit was regretting his sarcastic reply and felt the cold metal against the side of his head. He was in paralyzed by fear.
"Pull the trigger," said the doctor, calmly and slowly.
"Click!" Smit heard loud clicking noise which penetrated through his brain like an invisible bullet.

Now the scary one loaded the bullets into his Luger pistol and raised his arm to take aim at Smit.
"Give us names!, and we shall grant your freedom,"
Smit simply did not know what to do now and began to shake with fear.
"Stand up and take off *all* your clothes"
Smit stood up and his body seemed to creak as he grimaced in pain. He began to undress. His clothes were hanging loosely on his long lanky frame due to his weight loss from lack of food.
When he finally dropped his underpants to the floor, he looked down at his pathetic body. He was as thin as a rake. The scary one, walked forward and threw a punch at Smit, hitting Smit in the ribs. Smit leant forward and then felt another kick in the groin, which brought him to knees as he groaned in agony. The doctor planted the heal of his boot onto Smit's back, causing Smit to roll around on the floor. For the next minute or so the kicks came from everywhere, he clutched his hands around his head, and curled up in a ball, he prayed this would all be over. It seemed to have stopped, and then the short fat NSB man jumped two footed onto Smits skull. His world went black, and the room went quiet. As he rolled around on the floor he moaned in pain, in a semi-state of unconsciousness.

Gary S Smith

Smit prayed to God that this nightmare would be soon be over.
The NSB officer picked up Smit's clothes and they all left the room.
Once the echo of the slamming door had faded, silence returned to the cell like a familiar but ghostly friend. Smit looked down at his body. His nakedness was not just physical. He felt humiliated, weak and ashamed. Smit sat cross-legged on his bed and began to shiver. At that moment it seemed clear to Smit that all he had to do was write down one name, and maybe, *just maybe* the torture would stop. The cold damp room offered no warmth. He opened up the sheet of paper and began to weep, at first silently, and then loudly and uncontrollably.
His blood stained right hand was shaking. He looked at his hand again and realised the blood must have come from wiping his nose with his hand. Smit held the pen with his right hand and pressed the piece of paper against the wall with the back of his left hand as best as he could despite being hindered by his broken fingers. As his naked skin leant against the cold wall, his legs were still shaking from the trauma. Smit slowly began to write down the only name on his mind.
"*....Dirk Van Klooster*"

Five Days in May

Gary S Smith

CHAPTER FOURTEEN

TILBURG

"The world is indeed full of peril, and in it there are many dark places; but still there is much that is fair, and though in all lands love is now mingled with grief, it grows perhaps the greater."
– J. R. R. Tolkien

20th September 1942, Rotterdam.

It was Saturday, around 9.00 a.m. when Dirk boarded the train at a local station on the outskirts of Rotterdam (avoiding the main Rotterdam Central station). It was better that way, because he would have been recognized at Rotterdam Central by his work colleagues and drawn attention to his departure: or, more accurately, to his escape.

Dirk was desperate to leave his beloved Rotterdam. It was not safe for him now. Since Smit had been taken in for interrogation by the Nazis three days ago, it was only a matter of time before Smit would be tortured into giving names and details of their underground activities. The other members of the resistance cell, such as George and Frans were also at risk and it seemed certain that they would also hide or runaway somewhere. Nazi torture methods were known for being brutal, and successful. In terms of escape and hiding, it was everyman for himself now. It also made no sense to openly share their individual plans for escape, for obvious reasons.

He had posted a note through his neighbour's door along the lines of *"Gone to Eindhoven for the weekend"*. Dirk had quickly packed a small brown case which contained some essentials. Mainly;- his waterproof coat, some biscuits, chocolate, a lump of cheese, a bottle of whiskey, cigarettes and his leather walking boots. Dirk's plan was to buy a ticket to Eindhoven but to get off the train at an earlier stop closer to the Belgium border at Tilburg. Tilburg was a Dutch town around five to eight miles from the Belgium border. From there he planned to walk or cycle across the border. After that, he would head towards England via Spain.

A surge of relief swept over Dirk as took his seat in the train carriage near a window and placed his case on the spare seat on his left . The train was almost full. The passengers consisted of an awkward mixture of Rotterdammers travelling into the countryside for the weekend, and German soldiers in small groups scattered around the carriage. Despite the presence of the Germans, Dirk was still, in theory, on familiar Dutch territory. By now, he had rehearsed his "reason for travel" alibi speech so many times that he believed it himself. He was going to Eindhoven to meet his parents.

There were four noisy German soldiers sat behind Dirk who seemed relaxed, smoking and drinking beer. They were in good spirits, chattering nosily, laughing about the poor quality of the Heineken beer. They started up a loud conversation about their individual sexual encounters with the local Dutch girls. Each soldier gave a sexually explicit and graphic account. The Dutch passengers, who understood the German language all too well were not impressed with this tactless arrogance. A woman sitting on her own to Dirk's left, caught Dirks' eye as she shook her head in disgust. Dirk was momentarily intrigued with this silent act of defiance against the occupiers. He looked over his newspaper subtly to gain another glance at her. It was difficult to tell whether the woman was in her 30's or 40's due to her floral head scarf, and thick rimmed glasses.

The loud German voices dominated the carriage to the extent that all other conversations had now stopped to listen in bitter silence. It was another example of the humiliation suffered by the Dutch during the German occupation. Dirk tried to contain his simmering rage by focusing on the distraction of the passing scenery visible through the train window. There was a regular conveyor belt of fields, hedgerows, small thin trees, and small farms. He was impressed with the continuous network of canals.
As the train moved further away from Rotterdam, he became mesmerized by the repetitive views of flat green fields passing by. It was scene of tranquility, untouched by the destruction of war. The cows became a curious source of interest. They either lay down basking in the sun or stood grazing on the flat fields. Dirk envied the simplicity of their existence. Although admittedly their existence was only for a limited duration, until they were ready for slaughter. He did not envy their one way ticket towards the slaughter house and butchery. The cows had no plan to avoid their fate. Doing nothing and standing still, was no escape plan for these gentle creatures.

Dirk's thoughts were interrupted by the train's imminent arrival at Tilburg. The train steadily grinded to a halt at the station, and there were only a few people getting ready to depart. One of these was the woman with the floral headscarf who had been sitting near Dirk. As he stepped off the train and onto the platform at Tilburg station he held open the carriage door as a mark of courtesy. As she stepped off the train the lady in the headscarf smiled.
"Goedenmorgen," said Dirk.

"Goedenmorgen," said the lady breaking into a smile. They had both seemed to forget that it was early afternoon.

"It's good to get away from that intolerable German arrogance. Those guys were not respectful," said Dirk quietly, looking around.

"Rude. Vulgar pigs," she said.

"May I carry your case ?" said Dirk.

"Oh, thank you, that's very kind," she said handing over a case of similar size of Dirk's, but much lighter.

They started to walk along the platform side by side.

Then she lowered her voice and turned to Dirk.

"God knows how many Dutch girls have been raped by these Nazis?" she said rhetorically.

They joined a small queue. Around six people in total. A German soldier was stood checking the papers of the passengers as they entered the small station building. He had a Schmeisser machine gun on his back, but he was not really looking at the papers diligently, he seemed more interested in looking at the individuals.

When it was Dirk's turn he tried not to look nervous and handed his papers over, and he also took the lady's papers at the same time assuming that they were a married couple. The German paused looking both at Dirk and the lady and smiled. Probably thinking that they were having an affair in the countryside. He handed the papers back and Dirk and the lady walked out of the station.

"They are looking for British RAF pilots," said the lady.

"Yes, you're probably right," said Dirk.

The town centre was neat, tidy and moderately busy. There was a bakery, a butcher and a shop selling tobacco.

Dirk stopped walking along the street and handed the lady's case.

"Thank you, you are a gentleman," she said. Removing her head scarf revealing her blonde pony tailed hair for the first time. She looked completely different and much younger, maybe around thirty. Dirk's heart skipped a beat.

It was a rare liaison with a woman. Since his wife died of polio five years ago, he had lost all interest in the pointless pursuit of finding a replacement. Emily was a childhood sweetheart who could not be replaced.
A cyclist rode past narrowly missing Dirk who was drifting into the road.
"Are you okay ?" she said.
"Yes, sure. I was miles away for a minute," said Dirk.
"I'm walking this way," she said pointing towards the street going southwards.
"Ah yes, me too," said Dirk.
They walked in silence, for a couple of minutes. It was a comfortable silence pleasantly interrupted by the rapturous bird song of blackbirds in the tree lined road.
"Are you staying in Tilburg? or are you going …… Beyond."
Dirk was reluctant to give details, but his gut feel was that he could trust this lady.
"Outside Tilburg," said Dirk putting his case down so he could light up a cigarette.
"Do you smoke?" said Dirk
"No thank you," said the lady.
They continued down the street and there was another pause.
"If you …wanted to go into Belgium from here, it's better to go down this road for about four miles then go over the bridge and turn left onto the small farm track for around three miles. It's quieter that way. It's also Safer and quicker as there is no border check point just a big dairy farm."
She stopped and shook his hand and smiled. Only the laughter lines and her conservative style of dress gave away her age but that did not betray her good looks and kind face. A strand of blond hair blew around her face towards her mouth and she elegantly brushed it behind her ear with her left hand. Both seemed to be hesitant and reluctant to part ways, but between them they could not manufacture enough conversation to avoid going their separate ways.

Five Days in May

"By the way. My name is Christina, and I want to help you…that is if you want help that is," She held out her hand.
Dirk looked down at his shoes and took his hands out of his pockets to shake hands with Christina. "Thanks, that's really kind of you. I'm Dirk."
"It's almost 2 p.m. already, only four hours until the curfew. It would be better if you stay overnight in Tilburg, and then you can make an early start and clear the border tomorrow and maybe arrive in France in a couple of days. It won't look good if you are seen travelling at night during the curfew."
"Okay, that makes sense, but do you know where I can stay in Tilburg," said Dirk.
Yes, I have a room above the café at the end of canal street. Let's meet in the cafe at 2.30pm. We cannot be seen here together, there are too many informers in Tilburg."
Christina turned and walked away down the hill, and Dirk Took out a cigarette as an excuse to delay his departure to labour his eyes on Christine's elegant figure sauntering down the quiet street. Her blond hair gently bounced around her shoulders in unison with each stride. But that was nothing compared to the hypnotic powers of those swaying hips. Not even Christina's conservative dress could suppress this alluring beauty. Dirk slowly walked towards the town centre in deep thought. He had not anticipated encountering a dilemma at this early stage of his journey.
Dirk didn't have a real plan of how to cross Belgium, into France. He had also discovered a welcome distraction in Tilburg. It was a gamble, but Dirk trusted Christina for reasons he did not know. Dirk reasoned that a delay of one day would not be problem, especially if his escape route to France was to be more organized.
It was only when he reached the café that Dirk realized that he had been walking for five minutes with an unlit

cigarette in his mouth. Ten minutes later he was inside the café drinking some fake coffee, but the company was real enough. It turned out that Christina owned the café. Over the next few hours, he discovered that Christina and himself had a lot in common. They had both lost their partners in the last few years. Dirk's wife Emily had died of Polio in 1937. Christina's husband, Karl, had been conscripted in 1941 by the Germans to work in German factories in Dusseldorf.

Christina closed the café early by flipping the closed sign round and pulling the blinds down. Some persistent customers still knocked and waited. Eventually Christina invited Dirk to the upstairs room where it was safer from curious customers. The candles were lit, and the radio was switched on.

"German music? said Dirk, with a smile that could not be seen in the semi-darkness.

"Well. It's better than silence," said Christina.

"I don't hate all of the Germans, not every single person of the seventy million German population; just the Nazis."

"Yes. Germany was a fine place with nice people. But then Adolf Hitler began to spread the Nazi virus and his people became infected. Now, most of them are brainwashed, and the rest too scared to resist."

Christina opened a bottle of French brandy and began to pour it into two glasses.

After a couple of drinks, they both began to relax, and talk more openly about their mutual grief. In Dirk's case for the first time, as he had never been able to talk to his friends or his daughter about Emily's tragic death. Dirk's approach for years had been to keep his feelings to himself. He had carried on as normal, sleepwalking on a diet of daily misery of living under a constant cloud of grief. But now it seemed natural to share his experiences with Christina, as she had been on a similar journey.

During the second bottle they spoke about the occupation

and their mutual hatred of the Germans, the NSB and the local informers. Christina was involved in the resistance somehow. They agreed not to share any details about what their roles in the resistance were, as this would be less of a burden if they were caught and interrogated later on. A map was spread across the table, routes out of Holland were discussed, with some contacts in France and Spain. But it wasn't all one way traffic, and when the bottle was nearly finished he made genuine promises about "coming back" to Tilburg one day, but for a longer visit this time, as the chemistry between them was mutually recognised. In the meantime, Dirk promised to write a letter when he reached London.

Half-way through the second bottle Dirk knocked his glass over whilst doing an impression of the local informer De Rat. Christina had fallen over backwards onto the bed in a state of drunken laughter. Dirk also slumped onto the bed falling into Christina's arms. An emotional and physical bond had been formed, and they held each other for what seemed like hours, but was probably just minutes. They tried to remove each other's clothes in a comical drunken way, but then gave up and frantically undressed separately to save time. The love making had been frantic to start with, and then more measured to savour the shared moment of rare pleasure in uncertain times. Perhaps it would be the last time in an era of 'here today and gone tomorrow'.

When Dirk left the café at 6 a.m. Christina was still asleep. He crept out of the back door and found the bike propped up outside where Christina said the bike had belonged to her husband, Karl. It was a beautiful sunny morning and the birds were singing triumphantly.
As Dirk set off on Christina's bike, with a rucksack full of food, coffee, French Brandy, French Francs, a map and a compass. He also had the name and address of a French

Gary S Smith

resistance contact stuffed into his shoe. Apparently they could arrange French identity papers for him. As Dirk cycled downhill out the town and into the rural roads, he was surrounded by views of lush green fields and hedgerow lined country roads. Then he free wheeled downhill with the sun on his back and the westerly cool morning breeze in his face. Away from the crumbling city of Rotterdam, Dirk was entering into a new world, and it felt different. It was the first day of his new life.

CHAPTER FIFTEEN

A GOOD SCOUT

21st September 1942, Rotterdam

It was the ninth day of captivity. Smit's naked body lay on his bunk in a fetal position, with his arms wrapped around his sides for warmth. Smit shivered uncontrollably as his body's defences tried to deal with the traumatic aftershock of the interrogation. There had been hardly any food and drink over the last nine days: only stale bread, some rice and a little water. Smit was drowning in guilt and humiliation as the piece of paper with Dirk's name on has been taken away yesterday. He stared at the black wall and contemplated his future, if he was released. Smit decided he would seek to dull the pain of guilt and humiliation through whiskey. His only plan was to drink through his foreseeable future.

Yesterday the short fat NSB man had visited his prison cell and had taken the piece of paper from him, and marched out quickly; his German masters would be impressed when he handed in the answer to the homework question. However, Smit could not see many benefits from freedom and survival. He would never establish true peace of mind as he was now a traitor. Smit had betrayed his closest friend and Dirk could be brought in for interrogation at any time, unless of course Dirk had *done a*

Gary S Smith

runner already.

The keys rattled, and the door opened. It was the older Gestapo man. The short stumpy 'doctor' who took large strides into the cell to make up for his lack of height.
He stood in front of Smit and handed a pile of clothes to Smit who slowly began to unfold the clothes.

"Guten Morgen Herr Smit," said the doctor adjusting his round rimmed spectacles.
Smit just nodded and began to get dressed quickly.
"I have some news for you. Good news for us, but bad news for you," said the doctor with his hands behind his back.
"Okay," said Smit fastening his belt around his reduced waistline.
"The good news is that we found *Selene,* the mysterious fishing boat that has been used to smuggle Jews out of Rotterdam. We also found the owner of the boat, the stubborn old man with the white beard. He would not talk until we reminded him that he had a family, and a Grand Daughter called "Selene" and then suddenly he began to be…more cooperative…. shall we say."
The doctor took a deep breath and continued.
"Unfortunately the old man was knowingly part of the illegal smuggling operation along with you and Mr. Dirk Van Klooster. The old man has now passed away, his heart was weak. He must have died of guilt."
The doctor put his hand in his inside pocket and took out a pipe, and placed it on Smit's bed.
"A departing gift, from an emotional old man. Such a generous old soul, don't you think."

Smit remained seated on his bed and stared at the wall without any facial expression.
"The agreement we had ……was that If I gave you a NAME then I would be granted freedom from your

captivity," said Dirk drily. His voice sounded rather weak as he hadn't spoken to anybody properly for days.

"Ah. Quite correct," said the doctor as he raised a finger to acknowledge the point, in a courtroom manner.
"That offer was made *before* we discovered the full extent of your involvement with the resistance. After a more detailed house search we found several guns and explosives in your back garden. Then the doctor lowered his voice to spit out the words.
"I could only imagine you intended to use these guns for a terrorist attack against the Reich?"
Smit looked up to the ceiling. The answer was yes, there was no need for confession or denial, besides he had not prepared a false alibi.

"God knows how many Jews you have smuggled out of the Netherlands to enemy territory. There is a heavy penalty to pay for such crimes, Smit."

The doctor, like a judge in a court of law delivered the sentence.
"So. Because of your fondness of the despicable Jews, in the future you will be spending more time living with the Jews courtesy of our purpose built camps. Now that you have confessed to your list of crimes you will be travelling North East by train …to a deportation camp in the Netherlands called Vesterbork. From this point on you will no longer be a threat to the Third Reich."

The doctor straightened his glasses and smiled. For the next few seconds he nodded slowly and continuously in satisfaction. His investigation had been successfully concluded. He tilted his Gestapo hat, spun round on the spot and marched towards the door.
"Oh. In one hour, *you will* depart these premises to embark upon your train journey."

Gary S Smith

The tears built up inside Smit and there was no need to hold them back. There was no need any longer to hide his emotions because the defensive dam had been broken. He held his head in his hands and wept. The tears firstly came intermittently and then continuously. Smit had thought he had bought a ticket of freedom by giving the Gestapo one name. The price of being a traitor was an expensive price to pay, but he could not stand the torture and the unimaginable pain any longer. Now he'd realised that his betrayal of Dirk had been completely unnecessary. The Gestapo were going to kill him anyway, because he knew that people sent to the "camps" never came back.
Smit considered that they may as well have killed him straightaway, nine days ago.
Smit's hands were shaking violently as he had decided on his next move. He had less than one hour, maybe forty five minutes. Smit felt like a failure. He had been conned by the Gestapo into betraying his comrade and mentor, Dirk. In Smit's early years his father had always criticized everything that Smit had done. Somehow it didn't break Smit's confidence, it just made him more determined.
As a soldier he had failed, as the Dutch army had surrendered after five days of fighting and Smit left the battlefield despondent and defeated. As the youngest member of the resistance cell, Smit was eager to impress Dirk by devising new schemes and plans to smuggle Jews out of the Netherlands, or plan sabotage on the railways. Most of Smit's ideas were dismissed by Dirk as being "too rash" or "too dangerous". The bitter pill for Smit was that Dirk had been right. Smit should have relocated the weapons from Smit's house to somewhere else, but he didn't, and now the realisation of failure hit him hard like a tonne of bricks.

Smit rubbed his bearded chin in frustration and started to pick the laces out of his boots. Smit looked around the

Five Days in May

room and decided to tie the laces to electric light cable above him. He applied his scout knowledge from his childhood to tie a firm knot and a noose. Smit got everything in place around his neck and stood on his tip toes taking the pressure off his neck. He smiled to himself because now *he was in control* for the first time in nine days, possibly his whole life. All of his life he had followed the instructions of other senior people. His cocky and confident persona was a primary part of Smit's character, but it was merely a front for his insecurities.

Smit might not have been the most successful member of the resistance, but he had definitely been a "good scout" and a good soldier. Smit was proud of his life changing decision and he smiled bravely to milk the final drop of pleasure from his tortured life. Gradually Smit's toes could no longer hold his body weight and the noose tightened around his neck, until he could no longer breathe, and the burden of betrayal drained away. Soon after, the door opened, and Smit was already dead. This time, Smit (and not others) had decided his destiny.

Gary S Smith

Five Days in May

CHAPTER SIXTEEN

THE RIVER MEUSE

21st September 1942, Belgium

Dirk cycled over the Dutch-Belgium border by taking a farm track through a forest. Like many land borders, there was no line across the ground. In fact, Dirk only realized that he crossed the border when he saw a road sign in French and another in German. As promised by Christina, the border was not manned, and Dirk was elated that he had now left his troubles behind him in the Netherlands. Dirk continued to cycle through the peaceful country lanes, with a new sense of freedom. The views of the beautiful country side swept over Dirk like a majestic spell. He only stopped for a break when his stomach needed food, which was the fuel required to cycle long distances. Dirk had lay his bike down flat in a field next to the road, and he sat under a nearby tree. Out of sight from the road, Dirk relaxed for the first time that day. He leaned his back against the tree, kicked off his boots and rummaged in his rucksack for a cheese sandwich. All he could hear, was the sound of grasshoppers and the buzzing of flies. Dirk's spirits were high, and he felt good in this heavenly paradise. Physically, he basked in the healthy satisfaction of slightly aching leg muscles. The idyllic scene was interrupted when a German soldier on a motorcycle roared passed. Dirk smiled, as he lit up a cigarette to celebrate his luck. As he exhaled the smoke he watched the motorbike gradually fade away into the distant countryside. There was no escaping the war in mainland Europe.

Dirk's plan was to head south east until he reached the River Meuse (the Belgium section of the River Maas) then he would follow the River going West through Namur and then finally to Chatelet, where he would meet a man called "Albert" who lived in a farm house on the south side of the River. Apparently Dirk *"couldn't miss the Farmhouse"* because it was painted white and had the name "Blanc Maison" on a brown picket fence, with a huge willow tree in the front garden. That was the information scribbled on a piece of information, signed by "The Red Tulip". This must have been Christina's resistance code-name.

Dirk cycled on, trying to maintain his south-west direction. The novelty of cycling began to wear off after 20km's, but he would not stop now until nightfall. Luckily the roads were mainly smooth, a bit bumpy in places and generally quite flat, so progress was good. The Belgium country side was mainly agricultural farmlands. Dirk waved to any farmer he met on his way, to maintain the traditions of countryside, but without engaging in conversation. Afterall, he was a Dutchman in Nazi occupied Belgium, without any Belgium or French papers. Dirk knew that if he was caught then they would send him back to Rotterdam, not to the Ritz hotel but to the Gestapo headquarters.

Five Days in May

Dirk embraced the peaceful solitude of travelling through picturesque country lanes, lined with their majestic hedgerows. Although it was Autumn, the weather was still warm. As the September sun started to go down he could feel the coolness on his fingertips, and the edge of his nose and ears. The long distance cycling during the day had kept Dirk warm. Dirk prayed for dry weather tonight, the last thing he needed was rain because he planned to sleep rough in a field. Until he reached the Belgium town of Chatelet, it was just Dirk and his bike sleeping under the stars.
The very thought of this made him peddle a bit faster. Dirk felt strong as he had cycled since the age of two and a half years old. In the Netherlands they said you can cycle before you can walk.

Suddenly a car, came speeding around the corner of a bend, heading towards Dirk. It was German staff car. Dirk tried to cycle a little bit more casually, as if not in a hurry. Unfortunately, the car screeched to a halt, and the passenger held up his hand to make Dirk stop.

"Bonjour Monsieur!" said the German officer, in a terrible French accent. He had a pistol in his holster.
"Bonjour Monsieur," said Dirk tipping his cap, playing the part of the farmworker answering to a superior.
"Où se trouve Tilburg ?"
"Ah, Qui. Suivez la route à suivre pendant dix kilomètres jusqu'au carrefour, tournez à droite. Alors continuez."
"Merci," said the German officer who nodded to the driver to continue.
The car accelerated and shot off down the road. Obviously in some kind of hurry to reach Tilburg.
Dirk peddled furiously forwards and built up a good speed on his bike. His stomach was empty again, he felt slightly sick, and the adrenalin was pumping. He had to get off this road somehow in case his new German friends decided, to

come back and shoot him for giving out the wrong directions.

The next five kilometres, was completed much quicker than the previous five kilometres. Dirk saw two fishermen walking north with fishing rods down a farm track that left from the road that Dirk was on. *"The River Meuse ?"* thought Dirk as he followed the farm track a short way which unveiled views of the River Meuse in the distance, with its small trees lining the river bank. There was also a path next to River that he could follow south. Dirk walked for a while with his bike. The river was oozing forwards, slowly but gracefully. It was a majestic sight, and the next chapter in Dirk's long journey. The blue water glistened in the low autumn sun, and large carp cruised near the surface. Dirk welcomed the change of scenery and began to walk with his bike along the well-worn path at the side of the river. The banks were lined with bulrushes that swayed in the wind. There was a smattering of over-hanging trees that provided some cover from the road, but not enough as he saw the occasionally car pass by. As Dirk mounted his bike and began to peddle, he started to whistle. He was on his way to Chatelet.
It was slower progress along the river, due to the varying state of the bumpy path. He passed several fishermen on the banks, who barely batted an eye lid towards Dirk trundling past on his bike. As the shadows grew longer Dirk stopped for water and calculated on the map that he had covered thirty Kilometres along the river. It was taking longer than road travel, but it seemed safer. The sun went down and Dirk began to scan the riverbanks for a safe place to spend the night. In the end, he opted for a perfect spot behind a hedge and he bedded down in the long grass of a wheat field. Dirk had some more cheese, bread and chocolate. He was ravenous, and his food supplies would not last long. As he lay on his back, head resting against his rucksack he gazed up at the stars. It was a cloudless night,

and Dirk used his coat as a blanket. After a few sips of French Brandy, the stars turned a little blurry and Dirk drifted off into a deep and peaceful sleep.

***

Dirk was awoken with the loud sound of a gunshot being fired. *"Jesus! What's that!"* Thought Dirk as he sat up rubbing his sleepy eyes, looking around him. Behind him he heard the click of a gun reloading.
"Hands Up!" said the voice of a man, in French.
Dirk put his hands up, still not being able to focus his eyes properly against the low morning sun
The man with a shotgun was short, plump, and he had a round face, with red cheeks. His trousers were held up by a belt made of rope, which his belly protruded over. He looked like a farmer, which was okay as long as he wasn't a Nazi sympathizer.
"Who are you and what are you doing in the middle of my field?"
"I'm ….a farm labourer…. just passing through on my way to Chatelet," said Dirk. His voice was weak and dreary. He probably didn't sound convincing.
"Looks like you are escaping from somewhere," said the man, who had a couple of dead rabbits dangling from his belt.
Dirk shrugged and didn't say anything. The gun was still pointed at Dirk accusingly. The man's eyes were bulging.
"For a start, you are wearing city clothes. You're the best dressed farm labourer I have ever seen. Even after a night sleeping rough in *my* field…..*you look like…shit, but in good clothes.*"
The farmer continued to point the gun at Dirk moving steadily closer, grinning wildly. Dirk looked at both barrels, and the man's bulging eyes were scary and showed intent. In contrast his nose was well rounded at the end, and it was red, like a clown.

"Okay, okay, I'm not a farm labourer. I'm a clerk in a railway office… from the Netherlands. The Germans wanted to send me Cologne for slave labour work in one of their factories…." Dirk held up his hands in submission.

"Dutch?" said the farmer, leaning on his gun.

"Yes sir," said Dirk.

"I'm not *very keen* on the Dutch. Stubborn, arrogant bastards. But that's *nothing* compared to these *Nazi bastards*. They *stole* my pigs, cows, and my old car. They even tried to rape my daughter."

Dirk noted that the theft of his pigs was mentioned before the rape of his daughter, and wondered if that was just a coincidence or an order of precedence.

He marched off with long strides towards the farm house, and after a few paces stopped and turned. "If you are hungry, you'd better come quickly with me, before somebody sees you."

Dirk stood up, checked that he hadn't left anything behind, slung his rucksack over his shoulder and followed the clown farmer across the field, like a farm dog following its new owner.

The clown farmer (Frederic), his wife (Josephine) and daughter (Angeline) welcomed Dirk into their farmhouse. As part of the introductions Frederic announced that Dirk was not a German spy or a local informer, and then everybody became more relaxed. It was a good hearty breakfast of Rabbit stew, three cups of fake coffee and homemade biscuit. It made a nice change to converse with people and actually sit down in a chair and relax. Two hours later Dirk left the farmhouse, his belly full and in good spirits. Dirk was also now wearing farm labourer clothes. Loose fitting trousers, a primitive belt and a long baggy cotton shirt. The hat was large and had a rim to

Five Days in May

protect him from the sun and rain. Dirk's ruck sack was now full of cheese, apples and ..a leg of rabbit. He had also exchanged his bottle of French brandy for some local wine. The stew seemed to swell around in his stomach as he walked along the river path. Dirk was walking now because he had given his bike away to the Farmer's daughter, Angeline. Angeline looked exactly like her father, short plump, round face and red nose. She even had the mad bulging eyes. The main difference was that she was wearing a dress and had long hair.

Dirk had been relieved to leave the farmhouse, as he had the feeling that Frederic was trying to marry him off with his beloved Angeline. Despite this social minefield, Dirk was alive and well, and the gun pointed at Dirk's head two hours ago had not gone off. There was also the advantage Frederic had shared some useful local knowledge about the river ahead to Chatelet. The rain clouds started to gather above, as the river flowed gently onwards. Dirk increased his pace and he continued his journey with renewed confidence.

The vegetation around the river became denser and more remote as it snaked its way nearer to the forest of the Ardennes. There was the occasional boat cruising by, and a friendly wave exchanged with the passengers without any questions being asked. As the rain came down there were less people to worry about as he plodded on. The fishermen on the banks were more interested in staring at the river, waiting for the fish to bite. After a few hours Dirk began to feel some hot spots on the sole of his right foot. He stopped and swapped his damp thin socks for a thicker pair, which were dry. He carried on as the rain came down heavier and some of the fair-weather fishermen began to pack up and leave the banks, only the hard core fishermen remained.

Gary S Smith

As Dirk continued his journey towards Chatelet, mile by mile, both feet became sore. The blisters were forming, and Dirk began to curse his feet, his socks and his poor quality boots. It was becoming painful to walk, and Dirk regretted leaving his bike as a present to Farmer's daughter. The riverside path was becoming smoother now and Dirk needed a bike, or to hitch a ride on a boat. The latter was riskier as there would be a lot of questions and that increased the risk of strangers becoming informers.

He tried to keep his mind off his feet, by thinking of Christina, but ironically he could not get Angeline out of his mind. After a few more miles his blisters popped and the stinging sensation in his feet was becoming unbearable, as he began to hobble and curse. Dirk stopped and sat down and began to peel off his socks which had become glued to his skin. If he had some tape, he could tape up his feet. He slowly put some dry socks on and laced up his boots and began walking slowly, painfully slowly.

When he rounded the next corner of the river Dirk noticed that two fishermen sat on the river bank facing the water had left two bikes resting against a hedge about five metres directly behind where they were fishing (In their blind spot). It was near a bridge. Conveniently the hedge was next to a road that came up to the river and over a bridge onto the other side. Dirk hobbled towards the bikes as he left the river path. He lifted one up, spun it round in the direction away from the river and jumped on and started to pedal. As he pedaled the bike seat began to bounce up and down and it started to squeak, it was the seat !, the springs were rusty. *Shit* !

As Dirk peddled on, he found his stiff legs were not as powerful as they should have been. Determination drove him on trying to push forward with his feet as much as he could. He felt the wind in his hair, and glanced behind, hoping the squeaking noise hadn't disturbed the fisherman.

Five Days in May

"Hey! that's my bike," came a loud shout from the riverbank.

Dirk stood up on the pedals, despite the pain in his feet he peddled harder than ever. He looked around to see a young man in pursuit, sprinting up the road fifty metres behind. The young man was going fast and running like a track athlete, long strides and arms motoring. He was getting closer. Meanwhile Dirk was peddling up hill, but struggling to move quickly and he couldn't see the top of the hill. The early evening sun was shining brightly in his face. He looked again, and he could see the young man was a teenager, wearing brown braces over his white shirt, puffing but still maintaining his sprinting pace. Now he was only twenty metres behind.

"Thief!" the young man shouted.

"How much do you want for the bike!" shouted Dirk in French as his hat blew off.

"It's.... for sale!" grunted the young man, now only ten metres behind him. *Maybe less.* Dirk could even hear him breathing now.

Dirk was panting hard, his face was red, heart racing and he could feel the sweat trickling down his forehead. The sun was blinding now, as if it was working against him. The gods were angry. Suddenly he reached the brow of the hill and his bike increased in speed as he was on a level.

"Sorry, ...but I need your bike because its ...an emergency," Dirk struggled for breath.

"Name your price ...for the bike," said Dirk.

"It's ....not for ...sale...its mine!" The young man said quietly and desperately, he was so close now, Dirk could almost smell him.

Suddenly, the road dropped into a steep decline, and Dirk's new bike began to pick up some serious pace.

"Okay, ...okay...you can have it for thirty francs!" the young voice was weak and flat.

Dirk raced down the hill with the wind roaring against

Gary S Smith

his ears. The Cool breeze soothed his hot and sweaty body.

Dirk looked behind to see the young man walking like an ape, almost doubling up through exhaustion.

"Thieving bastard!" he shouted.

There was a distance of eighty metres now, and Dirk stopped his bike and open his rucksack pocket to take out some cash, which he dropped next to the road, and then he jumped back on his bike and started to pedal slowly. He looked behind and saw the young man pick up the money counted it and shouted, "Hey thief! you gave me fifty francs !"

"That's right. Forty for the bike and ten for hush-hush!" shouted Dirk.

"You never saw me!" said Dirk

"Yeah, maybe" said the teenager, laughing loudly.

"By the way!" the boy shouted. "The back tire has a slow-puncture!"

"*You little bastard,*" thought Dirk. He peddled onwards towards Chatelet and smiled to himself. "*Just my luck*" he thought.

Five Days in May

Gary S Smith

CHAPTER SEVENTEEN

THE RED TULIP

22nd September 1942, Chatelet, Belgium

It was nearly dark when Dirk reached the outskirts of Chatelet. His only stop had been thirty minutes to fix his slow puncture (Christina had packed a puncture repair kit in his rucksack). The rest of the journey to Chatelet had been trouble free and for most of the final stretch he had been helped along by a strong westerly breeze behind him. No more walking for Dirk.

As Dirk got within a few miles of Chatelet, he could see the town in the distance and he began to scour the countryside for his destination. He passed several farmhouses, some were white, but none had a willow tree, or had a sign "Le Blanc Maison". He began to believe that he was looking for a needle in a haystack. Dirk eventually saw a huge Weeping Willow tree in a large garden backing on to the river. There was a brown picket fence at the front. Dirk opened the gate and limped along the garden path up to the door, wheeling his bike next to him. He knocked on the door, and an old lady, wearing an apron answered.
"What do you want?" she said putting on her spectacles to study Dirk with great interest.
"I'm looking for Albert," said Dirk, who has been hoping for a warmer welcome.
"You will find him at Villa Voisin. Follow the river path

until you get to the bridge. Cross over the bridge. Just head towards the tallest church steeple, it's on Church Street, Villa Voisin is number twenty-six, and it has a red door. Go quickly before nightfall, as there is a curfew at night and you will get in trouble," said the old lady who was already beginning to close the door.
"Thank you, and goodbye," said Dirk, who turned to leave and strode down the path. Dirk was busy repeating the old lady's instructions over and over again in his mind; so much, that he left his bike against the wall.

One hour later Dirk was sat inside the Villa Voisin, drinking cognac with three new acquaintances. Around the table was Albert, whose real name was Pierre. A British pilot called Tom Hughes and a middle aged woman known as Anna. Villa Voisin was a 'safe house'. As soon as Dirk had mentioned that the "Red Tulip" had sent him, Pierre completely relaxed and opened up the bottle of Cognac. Tom Hughes was a clean shaven Englishman, with a large pale face that looked even larger due to his combed back receding hairline. His journey towards baldness was premature and he was only twenty-five years old
Pierre continued to diligently top up the small glasses when they became empty. "Dirk, your French papers will take two days to *prepare*. You will become a French citizen, which is fine, as your French is good. Now Tom already has his papers, he is now a French man, but his French speaking is basic, and his French accent is *terrible*.
Anna will travel with you both by train to Corbie in France. Then we change at Amiens to go to Paris. We will stay in a safe house for one day, where others will join us. Then we go to Bayonne in South France. From there you will walk across the Pyrenees into Spain, San Sebastien and Bilbao. We will take another train ride down to Southern Spain until we arrive at Gibraltar. A British port and a British territory. From there we are safe, as long as the ship to England does not get sunk by a German U-Boat. There

was a pause as the people around the table tried to take in the magnitude of the epic journey that lay ahead.

"How long will it take?" said Tom, sipping his cognac.

"Maybe one week, to Gibraltar," said Pierre.

"What are our chances of success?" said Dirk, who was scratching at his unshaven face.

Pierre shrugged.

"I believe….around eighty per cent, based on our success rate to date."

"It depends on the guards on the train and at the station. A critical point is when the German guard inspects your papers, and this is where you are *on your own*. Its every man for himself. You need to look French, talk French, act French. Blend in and be normal. Do not attract attention by looking nervous. Look natural, *don't* look nervous."

"More bread?" said Anna, to break the silence.

"Yes please," said Dirk who hadn't stopped eating since he had arrived there.

Pierre stroked his long Belgium mustache.

"Remember, an important rule. If one person gets caught by the Germans…at the station when the papers are checked. Everybody else continues as normal. You keep walking and don't look back. We do not expose others by going back.

"Understood," said Tom. "That sounds easier said than done."

"I know, but if you get caught Tom, a British pilot will go to the POW camp. If Anna gets caught, or if Dirk gets caught they will be shot or tortured or both. The stakes are higher for us." Pierre delivered his statement in a practiced monotone. This was not his first rodeo.

There was a pause. Tom felt the discomfort of guilt. These people were risking their lives for him.

"If the Germans discovered this safe house, then Anna, me and Dirk would be tortured until we gave names, and others would be arrested and shot. If they caught nobody else they would pick ten random Belgium citizens in this town and shoot them, one by one, in cold blood. That's why not everybody wants to be involved with the resistance, …and that's why there is a large number of local people who absolutely hate the resistance movement. It does more harm than good. Is one British RAF pilot worth ten Belgium or Dutch civilians? they say," said Pierre as he finished his glass of cognac and placed the glass carefully on the table.

"Tom, you are also risking your life for the liberation of Europe every time you fly in your Spitfire across Europe. So, we are *all* taking risk. But I just want to remind everybody, the stakes are high if we get caught. Be careful and do exactly as Anna says, she is your captain when you make the journey."

***

Three days later Kobus, Tom and Anna boarded the train at Chatelet station, to begin their train journey to Corbie, France. The next stage would then be to Amiens and then Paris. At the station the checking of the papers was a long and tense process, and they nearly missed their train. Tom Hughes was the most nervous, as his French was just basic and didn't want to be drawn into a long conversation with the guards.

At Paris they visited another "Safe House" where others joined their group, including an American pilot (Buddy), a Polish soldier and another British pilot. For the next long stage of the journey (Paris to Bayonne) Anna had been replaced by Joel, a battle hardened French resistance man. They all swapped stories, and the British and Americans practiced their French language skills, whilst the others laughed at their attempts to learn new words. The days on the train were long and silent. The rattling of the train had a calming effect. But there was always *an edge* as most of the passengers were German troops, SS officers or French citizens. The latter category was an unknown entity, as they fell into three categories; - (i) actively pro-Nazi (ii) actively anti-Nazi and (iii) the silent majority who may have had an opinion but did not show it. The first two categories were dangerously inquisitive about Dirk, Tom and Buddy. Joel did his best to install his entire group of escapees in one train compartment for their group of four, where two would be facing the other two. This tended to shield the group from having to interact with the other passengers. However, whenever they changed trains, it was not always possible to sit the four men together, and that meant they would be sat next to strangers who might strike up conversation.

Fortunately, the questions were normally the standard pleasantries, such as good morning/how are you?/where you are going?/etc. Buddy's French was really limited beyond those questions, so his tactic would be to fall asleep. This resulted in Buddy either sleeping or appearing to sleep for the entire journey between Paris and Bayonne. Only waking for food, drink or toilet visits. This brought some mild amusement to the other three. Somewhere between Paris and Nice, Dirk made the mistake of giving up his seat to an old lady entering the train, and relocated himself in the only available seat, next to three German officers.
They were sharing a bottle of red wine, and soon produced a second bottle. After an hour of wine fueled German chatter, which Dirk pretended not to understand, he decided to focus on his French newspaper. When the chatter dried up, the singing started. At this stage they not only insisted on Dirk joining them in the drinking session, but also endless renditions of the "*Lily Marlene*" song. It was a relief when a young blond haired officer next to Dirk, fell asleep on Dirk's shoulder. It was a minor inconvenience, until the snoring started. Dirk looked round to his left and caught Tom's amused expression hidden quickly by the shield of a raised newspaper. Joel

Five Days in May

seemed to clock the interaction and he stared at Tom, who raised his newspaper a little higher, in defence. There were only a few notable events as the miles tediously accumulated. They were getting nearer to England, if not geographically, but psychologically. They were becoming more confident: Dangerously confident.
Joel their French resistance guide, chain smoked and read his Victor Hugo novel. Joel was five foot six, with light brown hair, side parted. His long mustache hid most of his facial expressions, however Joel only appeared worried on two events;- when one of the other three opened their mouths which prompted a wide-eyed *Joel stare*, and secondly, when Joel's cigarettes ran out.

The scenery became more rustic, as they travelled into southern France, which was very pleasant apart from the fact that they were in French Vichy government territory. Here there were less German troops, but more French citizens or French police that were pro-Nazi. Dirk did not believe that the sleeping Buddy knew where he was, apart from *Buddy land*. It was probably the safest place to be as the train rumbled on into Bayonne. The Pyrenees and Gibraltar would be different challenges.

Gary S Smith

Five Days in May

CHAPTER EIGHTEEN

THE CRASH

3rd December 1942, RAF Benson, Oxfordshire, England.

Three months after Dirk had left Tilburg, Kobus sat in the cold cockpit at 30,000ft as his Spitfire headed east towards mainland Europe on another sortie. Below him was the blue mass of the English Channel, littered with tiny boats that looked like sticks from this great height. Through his blister mirror he could see the low winter sun shining behind him like a fireball. The French coast line lay directly ahead. All around was a bright blue winter sky. Not a cloud to be seen. It was a privilege to see such as marvelous spectacle, Kobus felt good, apart from his hangover. The pub near to the RAF base, had become the social oasis of fellow pilots. Most of pilots were not married, and they enjoyed the attention of the local girls. Going to the White Hart in a blue RAF uniform seemed to be a social magnet (although most people wore a uniform of some sort). *There was a war on* and they never knew if *that* night in the White Hart pub, would be their last. Kobus had developed a taste for drinking scotch whiskey, on top of several pints of beer. This morning his hangover was still present, although a few puffs on his oxygen mask before take-off seemed to cure his headache.

As he passed over Caen's he climbed up to 37,000 ft, and a layer of frozen crystals began to form on the Perspex hood. Kobus shivered. It was bloody cold, and he prayed that his control dials in front of him would not freeze up. The high altitude was necessary to be invisible from the ground. Stealth and speed were essential. There was no point in attracting attention by flying low. His reconnaissance target was Den Haag (The Hague). The political and legal centre of Holland. He looked downwards and saw that thick base of cloud below gave him some cover from anti-aircraft guns on the ground. Kobus looked at his map, to check his course. He started to hum the Glen Miller tunes. It always helped to maintain his focus, and his spirits.

He continuously looked around for enemy aircraft. That was the main part of the job. Avoid attention. *Don't get jumped.* Kobus knew that without radio or guns he was vulnerable. It was a very lonely job.

Very soon, he would be over Den Haag and he swooped down lower to find his photographic target. At 25,000 ft he saw the puffs of AAK smoke below him, and then he heard the exploding shells close by. *They were firing at him.* One landed so close his plane shook and the shrapnel ricocheted around his plane.

'Shit! that was close," said Kobus, as he swung his plane to the port side, to alter his course. *"Move around, sharp turns, left and right"* he thought.

With the distraction of enemy flak, Kobus had lost his bearings. He fumbled for his map that was resting on his knees, as he tried to control his plane. He banked sharply to the left, so he could see below, and saw the long yellow stretch of Scheveningen beach. From above, the yellow sand looked like a beautiful sight, and Kobus briefly reflected on previous family visits to the seaside. It was one of the few times his strict Calvinist father, allowed Kobus and his brother to run wild and have fun. They played on the sands, enjoyed ice-cream, and splashed around in the sea. Scheveningen was only one hour on the

Five Days in May

train from Rotterdam, but for a small boy, the train journey was exciting, and the long sunny days seemed to last forever. It was always a big adventure for an eight year old. But now as a twenty-eight year old he was embarking on an adventure (with a 2% fatality rate). *Concentrate on the job, Kobus. Get those photos and get back home in one piece.*

Kobus spotted his target. A large factory making German war machines. He banked a little to the left to get a good look and straightened up and waited until his nose was over the factory. He clicked the camera buttons which lay in front of him in the place where the gun-sights would have been. A reminder that a reconnaissance pilot, had no need for gun-sights if there were no guns on the plane. "Click-click-click-click," his camera was his gun. *Oh no,* there was some low cloud, partially obscuring his target.
Kobus, against better judgement, did a second run over the target. The cloud cover seemed heavier, now. *"To hell with it,"* thought Kobus as he turned around and banked to the left for a final run over the target. *This was suicidal, you're not supposed to do more runs!* He reached out to the silver box and clicked the fire button on the camera. It clicked. Kobus turned around to head for home, and he checked his mirror to see if he was leaving vapour trails to his rear …and spotted a German Junker 88 on his trail about 600 hundred metres behind him. Kobus threw the throttle back and climbed up immediately. Climbing fast brought out the best and the worst of the Spitfire (no plane could climb faster than the Spitfire, but there was a tendency for the engine to stall, which could prove fatal in this case).
*Up, up , up, 32,000ft, ….33,000 ft…..*Kobus checked and the JU88 still followed him….*come on now, 34,000 ft…35000ft.*
Then Kobus banked steeply to the west, checked his mirrors, *nothing there !* he rubber-necked to look behind him. *Definitely nothing there. thank God.* The Spitfire was too fast for the Junker.

Gary S Smith

Kobus continued his journey back home to Oxfordshire. Thankfully, this was uneventful. He stayed at 35,000ft, and gradually came lower as he crossed the channel. Kobus noticed that his fuel gauge was showing that his fuel was much lower than normal. Taking evasive action burnt up fuel, *but surely not this much*. As he flew over the countryside of Hampshire and Berkshire, he noticed some trails of smoke coming from his engine. "Oh, for God's sake!" said Kobus as he maintained a straight course low over the fields of Oxfordshire. He had no radio, so he couldn't warn the base that his engine was smoking. The smoke was getting worse. He switched off his oxygen supply as he was much less than 5,000ft, and right now he didn't need any more flammable materials on his aircraft. At the same time, he seemed too low to bail out in a parachute.

Kobus dipped down to RAF Benson, and he could smell the leaking fuel as he was coming into land the smoke was now obscuring his vision. As he touched down he could see the airbase fire engines racing towards him on the runway. The Spitfire came to a halt, and Kobus wrestled to push the Perspex canopy up. He pushed up with both hands *come on you bastard!* It seemed to be stuck and wouldn't open. For a second it was jammed, and then the cockpit hood came up. The aircraft was now engulfed in flames and black smoke, and Kobus coughed on the black smoke. Somehow Kobus hoisted himself up with his hands which felt hot, he got a leg out and jumped onto the runway, catching his left leg on the wing on the way down, catapulting Kobus head first to the ground. Kobus heard muffled shouts and felt his face drag along the runway floor. A fireman dragged his smoking body from the burning plane.

Later on, that night there would be a spare seat in the White Hart pub.

Five Days in May

CHAPTER NINETEEN

BACK DOWN TO EARTH

4th December 1942, Oxford, England

When Kobus woke up in hospital his head was sore, and his eyes tried to adjust to the environment around him. He felt warm, as if his skin was burning. Bright sunlight filled the long narrow ward, reflecting on the white cotton sheet laden beds. Kobus counted twelve beds on each side of the ward. The long dark curtains were draped either side of the tall stately windows. Black-out curtains were a way of life in Britain, to reduce the chances of the building being a target for enemy bombers. There was a war going on, and nobody knew how long it would last.

The beds were two metres apart, and most were full. Some beds were curtained off, but Kobus was not well enough to feel curious about others. He felt tired and drifted in and out of sleep. Every now and then he heard the odd murmur of a patient or the footsteps of nurses walking up and down, which reminded him of his whereabouts.

The man in the bed next to Kobus was snoring loudly, but it was not a problem as Kobus could have slept through an earthquake. It was a low rumbling snore, like a freight train. The smell of disinfectant, bleach with a blend of urine filled the air. Kobus had plenty of time to take in his new surroundings, as the nurses were rushing back and to.

When Kobus awoke again he felt the smouldering heat

from his burnt skin. He had the irresistible urge to scratch his itching left arm and left shoulder. He touched the bandage across his forehead, and felt his cheek, which was heavily grazed. Kobus's mustache was probably still there, and he stroked it meticulously to check that it was really still there. But his lip felt numb and swollen. "*What a mess,*" thought Kobus. He remembered the crash on the runway at RAF Benson. An engine fire and burning cockpit was a pilot's worst fear. For many it resulted painful and horrific death. He had always dreaded this: much more than crashing into a forest or the Sea. Kobus had evaded death and in later years he would understand that he was very fortunate to survive such an accident. Again, the itching sensation was overwhelming. It made Kobus squirm, and wriggle around in his bed. Kobus thought about using the pull cord to get the nurses attention but didn't. It looked like there were others in the ward who were in a far worse position than Kobus. He saw a bed being wheeled passed him, the patient had a missing leg. *A bomb or an amputation?*.

Kobus layback on his bed and began to study the cracks on the high ceiling, the wobbly lines looked familiar. Could it be an Ariel map of a country. Kobus had survived the crash. He was alive. He wondered if his friends in the Netherlands like Dirk, and his brothers and sisters were alive. He wondered if his father was still conducting his religious ceremonies in his church and if his mother was still baking those marvelous cakes. Kobus wondered when God would intervene in this war and join the allies against the evil axis powers. The emptiness of atheism was appealing, but admittedly, the belief in a God gave people some hope for *something* to cling to.
There were stories of Nazi cruelty in occupied Holland, young men being taken into slave labour to support German factories and people being transported to mysterious camps. Kobus had no regrets about leaving his homeland, and he had settled well in England. Moreover,

he was doing his bit for the war and liberating the Netherlands by joining the RAF. One day he would go home, and his parents might actually be proud of him. The runt of the litter *came good* in the end.

Kobus's thoughts were interrupted by a voice.

"Good morning, Flying officer Van Hooten, and how are you today?" said a female voice.

"I'm okay thanks, a bit itchy and sore, …..but ready to go the White Hart pub tomorrow," said Kobus in a croaky voice.

"Not so fast, Flying officer," said the nurse smiling as she studied his chart.

"You have received a high degree of severe burning on the left side of your upper body. You also have concussion, which should ease off, but your fractured hip will take longer to heal."

Kobus watched the nurse go about her observations and studied her. Shoulder length dark hair, soft white skin, with a round kind face.

"I will change the dressing on the burns, and that should cool you down a bit, and then you'll get a heavy dose of morphine."

"Nurse Moorcroft?" said Kobus reading her name badge.

"Elizabeth," corrected Elizabeth, in that authoritative English headmistress style.

"…Elizabeth, just like the British *Princess Elizabeth* ?" said Kobus.

"Yes, that's what all of the soldiers say. But the RAF patients are normally more sophisticated than that," said Elizabeth playfully.

Elizabeth had thrown down the gauntlet. *"From now on whatever I say will be original and witty,"* thought Kobus.

Elizabeth finished taking Kobus's temperature, and held his wrist while she took his pulse. Kobus enjoyed the tender feminine touch.

The moment was broken, with the arrival of Flying officer James Gordon.

Five Days in May

"Hello Vanny! How are you doing old chap, looks like you're in good hands, lucky blighter," said Gordon clutching a bottle of Scotch Whiskey, raising his eyebrows slowly and tilting his head towards Elizabeth.

"Hello James, Bravo," said Kobus trying to sound equally upbeat. Kobus looked at the bottle of whiskey. The thought of drinking whiskey made him feel sick.

"I'll leave you gentlemen to catch up, and then we'll get those wounds changed *Kobus*. Thirty minutes." Elizabeth nodded to confirm the deadline and turned and walked over to the next bed, the snoring patient who looked like he was completely covered in bandages, from head to toe; like an Egyptian mummy.

Elizabeth said 'hello' to her next patient, but the patient just murmured a low response through his bandaged face. Only his lips moved, and the sound was barely audible.

"I wonder what happened to that poor man," said Kobus.

James leaned over the bed, getting closer to Kobus and whispered into Kobus's ear.

"He was the firefighter who dragged you clear of your burning Spitfire."

Kobus swallowed hard. His throat was suddenly even dryer than before.

"But why …is he…worse than me?"

"When you jumped out the spitfire, you must have hit your head and passed out. He ran up to the aircraft and dragged you along the ground to get you away from the burning Spitfire. Then he …unfortunately became engulfed in flames. A human torch. Another fireman and some others threw their jackets over him, and you to douse out the flames but for him … the damage was already done. Your camera film was destroyed, as the film is highly flammable, so nothing went to Mendenham for the PI team to analyse…bloody shame after risking your life for …"

Kobus had stopped listening and the itching sensation on his shoulder had returned with a vengeance.

Gary S Smith

James continued his monologue about the heroics of the RAF, the missions and the shenanigans of the White Hart, while Kobus rolled his head to one side and pretended to listen to James whilst he stared at the fully bandaged mummy man.
"What was …I mean…is his name?" said Kobus quietly.
James shuffled on his chair, and leaned forward towards Kobus, "I don't know his full name, but back at the base they call him Ned."
"He'll get a bloody medal for doing what he did," said James.
Kobus gulped, and nodded silently. He looked over towards the whiskey bottle, perhaps he would take a drink of firewater after all.

Five Days in May

Gary S Smith

CHAPTER TWENTY

THE CRACKS ON THE CEILING

4th March 1943, Oxford

Kobus lay flat in his hospital bed and continued to stare at the cracks on the ceiling above him. The cracks had formed several possible images, including a map of mainland France, and more recently: Elizabeth's face. A sortie over France was known as a "milk run" amongst the RAF reconnaissance pilots, because it was closer, and (in theory) easier and often these missions were allocated to new pilots. The intermediate and more challenging "dice runs" were the low countries of Belgium and Netherlands, and the most difficult operations were Germany, for obvious reasons. During his twelve weeks in the same hospital bed, Kobus had plenty of thinking time, while the doctors slowly patched up his skin and mended his broken bones. Too much thinking time, and the inevitable soul searching. The long hours of being bed ridden seemed to open the door towards negativity and constant self-evaluation . *Was Kobus a good pilot?*, well I guess he must have been good as he had been selected for most of his missions over Belgium or Holland, and some over Germany, such as Essen and Wilmhaven.

His duration in hospital had been extended to four months as his wounds had become infected, and his wound dressings needed regular changing. However, Kobus was stronger physically and no longer dependent on regular

Five Days in May

doses of morphine to kill the pain. The upside of this was that he had got to know Elizabeth very well. She was kind, attractive and had a good sense of humour. Some of Kobus's jokes had actually worked, especially the rude ones. Elizabeth had even laughed at some of the bad jokes and this gave Kobus some hope that his magic was working. Elizabeth seemed especially impressed with the fact that the Dutchman could speak English, French and German besides his native Dutch language. English people were always easily impressed with a person's ability to speak more than one language. Elizabeth had eventually agreed to go on a date with Kobus when he was finally out of hospital, provided they could go dancing *and it wasn't at the White Hart.* Kobus was in love, *or was it lust?*. Quite frankly Kobus didn't really care, whatever it was, it felt good. Kobus drifted off to sleep, this time with happy thoughts. His dreams were usually the same themes either individually or a combination of;- his childhood in Holland, previous reconnaissance missions or …his current mission …Elizabeth.

Kobus was in the middle of one of these dreams when another nurse (..not Elizabeth) was waking him up.
"Flying officer Van Hooten, you have a visitor," said the nurse.
Kobus opened his eyes and sat up in his bed rubbing his eyes. Stood at the end of his bed, was a man with a large pale face, in RAF pilot uniform. Kobus did not recognize this pilot.
"Flying officer Van Hooten?," said the pilot standing upright, hands behind his back, as if he was about to give a formal speech.
"Hello," said Kobus, still trying to place a name to the moon faced gentleman.
"My name is Tom Hughes…Flying Officer Tom Hughes, and it is with my greatest pleasure to hand deliver a letter from your Dutch friend, Dirk Van Klooster ?"

"…Dirk? … is he alive?" said Kobus in such a loud voice, sitting upright as if he was getting ready to leave his bed.

"Oh yes! he is very much alive and well, and he's in London waiting to meet you. By the way he is a very nice chap…"

"..That's great news! does he still look like a Hollywood film star with that slicked back hair?"

Elizabeth brought two cups of tea on a tray, with some biscuits, which she fussily arranged on the plate, whilst eavesdropping. For the next hour Tom gave Kobus the full story of their escape from Belgium to England.

Kobus read the letter quickly and with great excitement. He would meet up with the Dirk and Tom in the near future at a pub called the Seven Stars in the city of London.

Once the tea and biscuits had been devoured and the stories exchanged. Tom leaned closer to Kobus so none of the other patients could hear.

"There is one other thing, that I need to tell you."

"Tell me," said Kobus.

Tom's breath wreaked of garlic, but Kobus did not care.

"When we returned to England, it turns out that Dirk has a lot of information about the Dutch resistance, and local information about future strategic targets in the Netherlands, which the British Intelligence is *very* interested in."

Tom raised his head, looked around, and then continued.

"It's called the SOE, The Special Operations Service. They have already had several meetings with Dirk …and the SOE want to meet *you* also."

"Okay. I'll be there for sure. I'm out of hospital in three days, and then I have garden leave for two weeks, oh….and a date with Elizabeth." Kobus cocked his head in the direction of Elizabeth who just happened to arrive at the bed, looking at her watch.

"You lucky blighter!" said Tom raising his eyebrows.

"She's a great catch. You didn't waste any time in here

Five Days in May

then Kobus… you old rascal.." Tom gave an exaggerated wink.
Elizabeth was approaching Kobus's bed looking at her watch. Kobus held his finger to his lips, to tell Tom to stop talking. Tom stood up quickly, smiled at Elizabeth and gave an awkward bow. Then he waved at Kobus and scuttled off down the corridor, as if he just remembered an urgent appointment. Kobus sat up in his bed again, smiled and shook his head at Tom's dramatic exit. He began to think about Dirk and his young companion, Smit.

Gary S Smith

Five Days in May

CHAPTER TWENTY ONE

THE SEVEN STARS

"All we have to decide is what to do with the time that is given to us." – J.R.R. Tolkien

10th July 1944, London

The long awaited reunion of the two Dutchmen had been delayed due to the SOE's interest in Dirk's valuable knowledge of the Netherlands. Tom had proudly selected the "Seven Stars" pub, as it was named after the seven provinces of the Netherlands and was given this name to attract Dutch sailors in the seventeenth century. Kobus and Dirk were not very interested in the venue's long history, but thanked Tom for setting up the rendezvous.

The mood in the pub was upbeat. It was one month after D-Day and the allies had been pushing the Germans further back into Western France. There was a feeling that the tide had turned in favour of the Allies. Kobus and Dirk were more interested in catching up on their recent history. Kobus made jokes about Dirk's film star looks and his smart tailored suit. Dirk had commented that Kobus had lost so much weight that even his mustache was smaller. Both men had undertaken a long journey to travel from Rotterdam to London. It wasn't just a physical journey but an emotional departure from their occupied and tortured homeland. After all the jokes and the black humour had been exhausted, they became more reflective. It was also their fourth pint.

"Tell me Dirk, do you miss the Netherlands," said Kobus.

"No. The Netherlands in 1944, is not the same Netherlands before the invasion in May 1940. It gets worse by the day. Smit is a good example of the tragedy of the lives destroyed by war. He joined the Dutch army which capitulated in five days in 1940. Then joined the resistance to continue the fight to protect the Dutch people. Smit arranged the hire of a boat to smuggle Jews out of the Netherlands via Rotterdam, and he helped to save the lives of many Jews. Then he gets a little bit complacent and subsequently attracts attention from local informers. Then he is thrown into jail and tortured by the Gestapo for nine days. They found him dead in his prison cell. Suicide, but they might as well have murdered him after the extensive torture. He was like a younger brother to me."

Kobus grimaced and shook his head in pity.

"Back in Rotterdam, I was really quite tough on young Smit, I was only trying to groom him into a resistance leader and that involved ditching a lot of his ideas. Unfortunately, he always seemed to take criticism to heart, but I was just trying to protect him and reduce the risk of being caught. Smit held on through nine days of Gestapo torture before giving information that blew open our cell of four men. Those nine days allowed George, Frans and me to escape from the Netherlands," said Dirk, as he paused to take a long sip of his beer before rubbing his eyes and composing himself. The other two men watched Dirk silently, waiting for him to compose himself and continue.

"Smit was a bloody hero... deserves a medal. They must have messed him up so bad to force Smit into killing himself...I'll really miss him. I never had a brother, but I

feel like I've lost one now," said Dirk.
"The young lad, must have gone through hell, said Kobus quietly.
Dirk nodded and they said nothing for a while.
Dirk continued but could not shake off the sadness in his voice. "Now there are serious food shortages because most of the food is sent to Germany or further East. There is increasing brutality, repression, curfews, German soldier's everywhere... they treat the Dutch like *animals*; rape, torture and random massacres of civilians when they find local resistance activity. Thousands of people are transported to concentration camps or German factories for slave labour. The stories are true. But it's getting worse, and now none of the Dutch trust each other. You know: *who* is resistance? *who* is an informer?"
"The sooner we get *our* country *back* the better," said Kobus as he raised his pint glass.
"Prost!" said Dirk.
"Here's to the liberation of Europe!" shouted Tom, as the three men clinked their pint pots together, Tom spilled his beer over Kobus's sleeve in the process. But nobody seemed to mind.
Dirk discussed his meeting with Christina and Kobus spoke about Elizabeth in a gentle openness that was not normally possible between sober men. Everybody was already planning for their lives "after the war."
Tom Hughes had been listening politely and had insisted that they spoke in Dutch so that they could express themselves quickly, and not compromise the communication just for Tom's benefit. Tom waited for the pace of the conversation to slow down, Tom interjected.
"Hey Dirk, old chap. You know that the British SOE will want to extract all of the valuable local information that you have on Rotterdam and other such places?"
"Sure, I'm already in contact with them. I am glad to help," said Dirk.
"Just be careful now. They might try to recruit you as a

British/Dutch agent, and drop you back into Holland, which might be a bit hairy,"
said Tom taking a sip of his beer. Tom was beginning to slur his words, and his thin strands of hair on his forehead looked out of place. Tom wasn't a big drinker.
"I don't mind, I'll do whatever the Dutch government and the SOE ask me to do. If I can play my part towards the liberation of Holland, then I'll do it," said Dirk, a bit too loud. Some people on the nearby table glanced over.
Tom lowered his voice. "But, you've already done a lot for the Netherlands by smuggling dozens of Dutch Jews to safety in England, and providing the SOE with valuable information."
Dirk leaned forwards hands on the table clutched together, he felt that Kobus and Tom were being overprotective.
"The SOE have already helped to secure the safety of Frans and George. For me, I can look after myself, for sure. I know there are 'risks' if I go with the SOE or even if I go back and join the Dutch underground, there are risks everywhere. The main thing is that after the war, I have Christina waiting for me in Tilburg, and of course my daughter who is living with her grandparents in Eindhoven." he firmly placed his hands palms down on the table to indicate that the conversation about his safety was over.
"Kobus, what about you? What is your plan?, I see your keeping your cards close to your chest again.." said Dirk as he leaned back in his chair as a sign of waiting for Kobus to start speaking.
"Actually, I'm *not* going back to the Netherlands after the war. My plan is to live in England."
"…what? warm ale and bland food," said Dirk.
"…It's not warm ale, its room temperature actually," said Tom playfully.
"Okay now listen to this," said Kobus who was also starting to slur his words.
"Please… keep this secret, but Elizabeth is pregnant…and

we will be getting married in England."

"Congratulations!" shouted Dirk shaking Kobus's hand vigorously.

"Well done old chap! You certainly didn't waste time there," said Tom patting Kobus on the shoulder.

"Thanks, its really good news, She's a great lady, and my future is here now," said Kobus.

"You're a lucky man, Kobus," said Dirk who now was longing to meet up with Christina again more than ever.

As the excitement of the news began to simmer down, a man entered the pub making a bee line towards their table. He was wearing a trilby hat and a light brown rain coat as he entered the warm and stuffy room.

The man sat down and took off his hat and lit up a cigarette. He left his raincoat fastened.

He looked around the smoke filled pub, before speaking, and leaned closer to deliver his well-rehearsed speech.

"Gentlemen allow me to introduce myself, my name is Albert Greenway from the British Secret Service. We are known as the Special Operations Executive (SOE) to be precise. I am in charge of special operations in the Netherlands. We involve Dutch agents and British agents, who work closely together to support the Dutch resistance. The main activities are smuggling British or Dutch out of the Netherlands to England, and disrupting German military. Everything, is and will remain confidential. Careless talk costs lives, you know."

Everybody nodded, and looked serious now.

"Tell me, do you have any knowledge of the Hoek De Hollande?" said Greenway unbuttoning his top button on his rain coat.

"I know it well, my father used to have a boat there," said Dirk.

"Excellent, old chap. Let's not discuss any more detail here and I'll buy the next round of drinks and allow you gentlemen to enjoy the reunion, whilst I go to my appointment. Dirk, I would like to discuss the "Hook" in more details at my office tomorrow, in Whitehall. Here's my card. Nine a.m. sharp?" said Greenway, it was more of an instruction than a request.

"Yes, I can make it," said Dirk sincerely.

Greenway was aged around mid-forties, portly build with an oval face. The round glasses gave him an academic look. His approach was very formal and business like. He had a classic English accent, with an additional precision on the 'r's.

Five minutes later Greenway brought a tray of beers to the table, and said farewell and promptly left the pub. He had been in the pub for a total of thirty minutes. The three men finished their beers and walked along Fleet Street towards the River Thames. The moon light reflected off the Thames but the rest of the city of London was in darkness, due to *the blackout* restrictions.

The two Dutchmen were slightly drunk, and emotional,

"Hey, Dirk I've known you for years now. Who could have predicted our future back then ?" said Kobus.

"Yes, you are still bad at hockey and still can't hold your beer," said Dirk. "Before the war, my biggest worry was what career I should take, to escape from my parents!"

They all laughed, but the mood was melancholia.

"Then on 10th May, the bigger worry was how to escape from the Nazis," said Dirk.

"Yes, you took your time getting here, Dirk?, four years, to be precise." Dirk bumped into Tom as he responded to Kobus.

"Yes, I took the scenic route, and had a tour of Nazi Europe."

"For your birthday I'll buy you a map so next time you take the faster route ….by boat from Hoek van Hollande!" said Kobus.

"We shall see," said Dirk.

They stopped walking as they reached the river, it was time for the three men to depart in different directions and say

Five Days in May

their goodbyes.
"Tom, thanks for looking after me in London," said Dirk
"It was a pleasure, I needed the drinking practice," said Tom.
"Give my regards to Elizabeth…and the baby?" said Dirk with wry smile.
As Kobus lit up a cigarette. Tom interrupted the conversation.
"Listen!"
They could hear the "put-put-put-put" noise in the sky.
"It's a buzz bomb!" said Tom, it was another name for the V-1 rocket.
The three men looked up into the darkness of the sky as the noise of the V-bomb got louder and louder….. "Put-put-PUT-PUT-PUT…"

The V-1 was a terrifying weapon. The rockets had a range of hundreds of miles and they were launched from Nazi occupied western Europe towards London. The huge V-1 rockets could not be stopped or shot down. The rockets came day or night, in any weather. It did not feel that the Allies were winning the war when the Germans could launch rockets from hundreds of sites spread over France, Belgium and Holland. Thousands of V-1 rockets had landed in London creating the destruction of 250,000 houses and claiming thousands of civilian casualties. Londoner's dreaded the "put-put" noise but the silent pause was feared even more, because that was the point they started to descend. When the noise stopped, they took five seconds to hit their indiscriminate targets, and people on the ground counted down the seconds with dread.

Gary S Smith

Five Days in May

CHAPTER TWENTY TWO

HOOK OF HOLLAND

01.00 a.m. 30th September 1944.

All was calm 30,000 feet above the English Channel as the Dakota rumbled across the dark, moonless sky. Inside the military transport plane sat twelve men in soldiers' uniforms. Six men on each side of the fuselage. All had blackened faces and round paratrooper helmets, with the requisite camouflage netting. Their mission was to destroy a V-1 rocket site in Western Holland. The site had been identified by the Dutch resistance as a huge military establishment launching V-1 rockets from the Hook of Holland to London. There was also intelligence that the military base was being used to store large quantities of ammunition and possibly the upgraded version of the V rocket, that Hitler had been promising to turn the war back in Germany's favour. There was enough justification to destroy this base.

The puffing noise of distant flak started, the men now realised that they were somewhere over occupied France. The pilot wore goggles to protect his eyes from any shattering glass from direct flak hits. As soon as the pounding of the flak started, Corporal McKenzie and Corporal Davis began to sing.

Gary S Smith

"Up to mighty London came an Irish lad one day, All the streets were paved with gold, so everyone was gay! Singing songs of Piccadilly, Strand, and Leicester Square, 'til Paddy got excited and he shouted to them there…"
(then they all joined in the chorus, including Dirk)
"It's a long way to Tipperary, it's a long way to go!"

The singing got louder as the men sang their hearts out. Vibrations shook the aircraft, but at that point nobody seemed to show concern and the singing continued.

McKenzie, the wee Scotsman, passed a hip flask to Private Roberts who was sat next to him. McKenzie was the stereotypical hard drinking Glaswegian. He had red hair, pale skin and freckles to match. Roberts was a quiet man from Nottingham, and despite his imposing six foot three inch stature, Roberts was strangely self-conscious and embarrassed by his towering height. It was if he did not want to be noticed. Roberts didn't go to the pub very often, he stayed in the barracks and he was an avid reader who always preferred his own company. Roberts was a demolition expert and he eyed the drinks flask with professional suspicion and then quickly passed on the flask to Dirk.
"Prost!" said Dirk, before he took a huge swig of the flask. He coughed. The whiskey was harsh and it stung Dirk's throat like fire. He passed the flask back to McKenzie, feeling slightly sick.
"You Dutch lads enjoy a drink, I see?"
"Yes, but normally Beer, Wine or Brandy."
"I would have brought all of that, but the kit bag wasn't big enough," said McKenzie.
"If you can teach me the words to the *"Tipperary"* song, I'll take you on a pub crawl around Rotterdam, one day…after the war, of course."
"That would be very nice. Can you pay for the ferry cost from Newcastle to Rotterdam as well?" said McKenzie.

Five Days in May

A young paratrooper, Mike Bentley, leaned forward with his arms folded.

"What's up Bentley?...." said McKenzie

There was no answer. Bentley just leaned forwards.

"You look like you've seen ghost," said McKenzie.

Bentley vomited on the floor. This raised a couple of laughs in the fuselage, but not from Dirk who was feeling sick himself.

"*Jesus Christ* man, you've puked over my leg," complained McKenzie.

Dirk raised a smile. He had got to know these men quite well over recent weeks.

Each man had a large kit bag, with food and ammunition. It was mainly ammunition, with enough to blow up a small town. Bren guns, Sten guns, and plenty of grenades and explosives. After three weeks training on Dartmoor, Dirk was familiar with all of this British equipment (and the pubs). The guns were impressive, compared to his ancient Austrian rifle that he had in the Dutch army in 1940. The discipline was very tight. The formalities and procedures were almost overbearing, but luckily there was flexibility for this special platoon being trained for the mission, so they were given some leeway. Dirk found that the friendliness in the British pubs was infectious. Everybody seemed inquisitive about "Holland" as the Brits like to call it, as the Dutch language was a mysterious dialogue, rarely heard before. To some extent he had become a celebrity with the locals. Dirk was now fully integrated into a close-knit team of comrades. The twelve men were under no illusions that the risks were high. It was a dangerous mission and not many, if any, would return.

The purpose of the mission was to be dropped by parachute onto the Hook of Holland, which was a town on the south west corner of Holland. The Dutch called it "The Hook" or in Dutch "De Hoek" (which means "corner"). They would land during nightfall and destroy a

V-1 rocket site situated in the middle of a forest and escape back to England by a boat. The plan was undoubtedly very ambitious: Kobus and Tom had told Dirk that he was crazy to agree to go on this mission. Tom had called this a "suicide mission." Those words had sometimes haunted Dirk' over the last twelve months. Dirk had attended Greenway's Whitehall office and decided to go on the mission as it was his chance to *do something* to strike back at the Germans, rather than hide or escape. He was denied of the chance during the five days in May 1940, due to the rapid capitulation of the unprepared and archaic Dutch army.

 Greenway had taken many notes about Dirk's knowledge of strategic locations in Hoek van Hollande and other Dutch locations such as Rotterdam and Tilburg. Further meetings in the SOE office had been set, each time with a larger audience of Intelligence gatherers making notes and marking maps. Dirk's knowledge of the Dutch railways was of particular interest. There had been many meetings spread out over three months in London. It really seemed as if Dirk's information about the Netherlands was highly valuable. It was a good feeling to "do your bit" as the English say. Especially if it helped the war effort.

The Dakota plane dipped down as it began to lose altitude. *"It's a long way to Tipperary!, it's a long way to go....It's a long...."*
"Quiet! men!" shouted Major Carling. "We are not far from our target."
The singing stopped, except for McKenzie who defiantly finished the verse, much to the amusement of the others. The flak had now stopped. It was a truce. The singing had worked it many ways. It took everybody's mind off the jump.
Dirk looked up. The red light by the door came on. That meant it was four minutes from the drop zone.

Five Days in May

"Stand up and hook up!" the dispatcher shouted.
The first on his feet was Corporal Davis. A young corporal at twenty-three years old, five feet six inches tall, broad shouldered, and had a round potato shaped face, with shaved hair. He had been involved in the war for five years and had transferred into the special forces one year ago. A former factory worker, and a talented street fighter, had never been out of his Lancashire mill town home town before the war. The war had allowed Davis to discover that he had a talent for killing Germans, especially in close combat. Knife attacks and hand to hand combat were his main strength. Davis had quickly realised that many Germans had panicked in hand to hand combat, whereas Davis seemed to keep his cool and enjoy the challenge of close combat, which suited his small bulky frame.
Dirk's legs felt weak as he struggled to stand up, and clipped his static line to the overhead cable, which ran the length of the fuselage. Everybody began to check their straps and pockets. *Check, check, check.*
"Stand by the door!" shouted the dispatcher. The men inched closer to the open door. The wind was roaring, and the fuselage was getting cold and drafty.
The Dakota began to slow down ready for the drop, when the flak started again with a vengeance.
All of the men shuffled forward with their huge kit bags awkwardly, like penguins.
Everybody was still waiting for the green light, "Come on, let us out!" said Bentley, echoing everybody's thoughts.
"Let's get the bloody thing over with," muttered McKenzie. Suddenly the green light came on, and one by one the lemmings went over the cliff.

Dirk was in line to be the fourth man out of the aircraft just after Davis, who was now at least fifty per cent awake. Dirk had never jumped before. The fear of waiting for the jump would be greater than the fear of actually jumping into the cold abyss beneath them. Dirk stepped out into the roaring darkness, and as he dropped weightlessly, he felt a sudden jerk as the parachute opened. As he floated down a rush of adrenalin swept over him, like never before. He felt his kit bag, pulling at his ankle, as he looked down. Firstly, he could see nothing all around him but the blackness of the night. The rushing wind of descent brushed against his ears. No flak, no airplane sound, all was good. As he looked down again he began to make out the landscape of a forest. Dirk placed his two feet firmly together as he saw tree tops beneath him. Suddenly he crashed through soft layers pine tree branches, which knocked him slightly to the left and Dirk braced himself for the impact of hitting the ground. His feet sunk into the boggy ground half way up to his knees. He gradually squeezed one leg out at a time, which involved getting covered in mud as he awkwardly untangled himself from the straps using his trench knife. Dirk wrapped up the silk parachute and buried it under a bush as best as he could, hoping the locals would find it to make use of the silk material. He started to walk stealthily on the field looking for the others. The darkness was thick, and he had no idea where he was.

Firstly, he found Bentley climbing out of a ditch, splashing around and cursing. Within twenty minutes eleven men were altogether, but no sign of McKenzie after a ten minute search. Major Carling advised the men that McKenzie would be picked up by the Dutch resistance and that we continue with the mission to make use of the darkness. Apart from McKenzie's disappearance the landing had been successful, and the men waited. The Dutch resistance group let off a signal in the dark. A torch, making a "V" sign. There were six Dutch resistance men who appeared in the darkness and their leader, wearing a beret tilted to one side of his head, introduced himself as Joop van Kerk. The seventeen men briefly shook hands, without any verbal communication. Major Carling did a quick inventory of equipment and explosives round up.

Five Days in May

Little was said, they knew the main objective and they were all ready to attack the rocket site. Dirk's role was to be the liaison officer between the Dutch resistance and the British paras, but he also itching to be part of the raid.

The parachute drop had been accurate, and the seventeen men only had five miles to walk across fields to the military base. The heavy kit bags, drainage ditches and winding forest paths slowed them down. It took two hours to reach the German military base. Van Kerk led the way through forest, narrow canal paths, more forest and farmers' fields. Van Kerk and his men knew every path, and the location of every German machine gun post. Some of those machine gun post that could not be flanked, had to be disabled, and Roberts, Davis and Bentley took the opportunity to use their knives to a deadly effect. In some places Joop van Kerk had already cut gaps in the fences or hedgerows. Eventually, the twelve men arrived at Staelduinse Forest, where the German military base was located. They huddled together behind the trees, talking in low voices.
"Major, most of the buildings are over there in the next forest. I believe the V rocket is most probably in that big concrete building, next to the railway track. The two brick buildings adjacent are storing lots of ammunition and most probably chemicals." Van Kerk took a final drag on his cigarette and smothered the fag dimp under his boot. All of the buildings were heavily camouflaged.
"Bravo, van Kerk, you've done a great job to get us here," said Major Carling.
The other men started to unload unnecessary items from their bags, leaving only explosives and weapons. They gave the food items to the Dutch men who hid them in a ditch. They knew that the local Dutch population were starving.
"Plant your explosives under the railway and the communications building. We'll take care of the rocket facilities. Dirk, we will meet you and other Dutch

resistance boys on the North side of the forest on the road."

"For sure Major, we will have a farm trailer truck waiting for you when you have finished the job in the forest," said Dirk.

"Take the guns and the mortar, into the truck and be prepared to give us covering fire. If we are not back from the forest in forty minutes…just go without us, everyman for himself."

Major Carling's ten men started to spread out and crawl towards the wire fence of the military base in the forest. Davis already had his knife ready. He had become numbed to the horrors of death and violence. Davis did not really mourn the death of his fellow soldiers, he just became thirstier for revenge.

One by one, German guards patrolling the buildings were pounced on from behind, knocked unconscious and their throats were slit. The para troopers moved slowly, and carefully as the Forest was quite dense. Dead bodies of the guards were dragged into the surrounding ditches by the Dutch resistance men. There was a ruthless efficiency in the work. As they crept around the perimeter fence it was all quiet around the military base. An unnerving silence prevailed for thirty minutes as the explosives were carefully planted all around the buildings.

Dirk, van Kerk and Jaap prepared the farm truck next to the road, ready as an escape vehicle. The other Dutch resistance men planted explosives all around the fringes of the forest to create maximum confusion and destroy as much property as possible before making their own way home across the fields. Telecommunication lines were also cut. They had placed bales of hay on the trailer, with a Tarpaulin cover strapped over for cover. There was enough room for eleven men (in the unlikely event that eleven men survived the raid in the forest). The trailer was loaded with Bren guns, Sten machine guns, and grenades.

They waited in darkness, looking out for German patrols, whilst checking their watches. Twenty minutes to get the job done, then twenty minutes to get to the farm truck. There was no room for error.

"It will only take twenty minutes for the Germans to block all boats departing the port," said van Kerk. The Hoek is a huge military base, so it is heavily guarded."

"What happens if the port is blocked?"

"Then we will go into hiding in the town and become "evaders". We have a few 'safe houses' where the Brits can hide and I have civilian clothes in the bags. The resistance is very strong on the Hook, we are proud that this was the first resistance group established in the Netherlands..."

Suddenly, there were German shouts of alarm coming from the Forest. Then a short burst of machine gun fire could be heard, followed by several other short burst. Dirk strained his eyes in the dark, it was almost impossible to see anything in the darkness. A couple of minutes passed by and there was still no sign of Major Carling and his men. They were still in the woods. These delays introduced a terrible, unspoken dilemma concerning their next move. How long should they wait for the paras? if they drove off too early the paras would be slaughtered. However, if they were already dead, then the three dutchmen would waste their lives needlessly, not to mention the recriminations for the local Dutch population living in the Hook of Holland.

Van Kerk stared at his watch, looking for an answer, the British had already been gone for forty minutes. Major Carling had ordered the Dutch resistance to abandon them after forty minutes. *That was the order*. Dirk nodded slowly and tapped his wrist watch with his two fingers: Jaap and van Kerk understood the signal. They took their positions slowly in the truck Jaap stepped into the back of the trailer underneath the Tarpaulin, Dirk sat in the passenger seat and van Kerk settled into the driver's seat as if about to go

Gary S Smith

on a Sunday drive, and then he turned the key to start the truck engine. They were ready to go (with or without the British paras).

Five Days in May

Gary S Smith

CHAPTER TWENTY THREE

STAELDUINSE FOREST

3.30 a.m. 30th September 1944.

As the key turned in the ignition the old truck engine reluctantly spluttered into life. The loud noise of the engine echoed into the night. Instead of going forwards to safety van Kerk reversed slowly down the road, towards the forest. The truck's engine noise was now overshadowed by awakenings in the forest. In the darkness there was a sound of a scuffle, a rumble of boots followed by a short burst of machine gunfire. Jaap peered out of the back of the truck, with his Sten gun pointing out from under the Tarpaulin. The only problem was that Jaap could see nothing to shoot at in the darkness. Only the flash of gun fire could be seen. Van Kerk slowed down the speed of the reversing truck to a gradual halt as he sensed they were near Carlings men, or even worse to the German patrol. Dirk had his Bren gun pointing out of the passenger window, and now he could hear the footsteps of paratrooper boots clogging onto the road. There were shadows of five British paras running up to towards the truck which had now stopped. "All of us are here, permission to fire!" said Major Carling rather breathlessly. The Major was giving the order whilst being carried by one man in a *fireman's* lift. This meant that five paras (excluding McKenzie) were dead or missing in the forest.
Two men lifted Major Carling onto the back, whilst Jaap gave covering fire from the back of the truck. The major

had been shot in the leg and was bleeding. The truck started to move forwards ever so slowly. However, it built up speed gradually. The four remaining paras started to crawl under the bales of hay grabbing their weapons and getting into position to fire out of the back of the trailer. Davis was covered in blood, uncertain if the blood was his. Bentley burrowed a hole in the hay, so he could see out of the back. Corporal Downs crawled towards the back and opened fire with his Bren into the darkness behind the departing truck. Roberts gathered up the ammunition and began to distribute this amongst the men. The paras seemed to be confident that German patrol who followed them out of the forest had been dispensed with. "Cease fire!" ordered Major Carling. Whoever was following them, did not seem to be firing at them anymore. For now.

As the truck continued its journey towards the coast a series of explosions erupted from the forest. The first was the loudest, the ground rumbled, and small patches of flames could be seen within the dense forest. Steadily the flames grew taller and more prominent. After a minute or so, the centre of the forest was alight with a crescendo of flames and sparks reaching far above the treetops. Some of the smaller debris landed on the road. The other explosions followed in different parts of the forest, and finally the air raid sirens from the military base started up. All hell was breaking loose.

There was a series of explosions from the heart of the forest with flames jetting up into the sky like a flamethrower hundreds of feet high. It must have been the chemical storage containers. The tightly packed trees around the base started to burn wildly into an inferno. Corporal Downs could see the distant silhouettes of soldiers fleeing into the safety of the night. The spreading fire set alight vehicles and fuel storage dumps. It was a large military base, with a huge content of supplies. In the centre of the forest the trees burned like matchsticks. The men in the truck were mesmerised by the colourful scenes of destruction before them, but there was no celebration as five paratroopers had been killed or lost in the forest. Fireworks and mini-rockets fizzed into the sky, as the flames ignited a German ammunition dump.

As they gazed at the spectacular chaos they had created, a fire engine passed them by. This was followed by a German BMW motorbike. Surprisingly the farm trailer was not stopped. There was no reason for the farm truck to be travelling at 4 a.m. in the morning during the curfew.
As the farm truck rumbled along the bumpy road they moved out of the forest area into a flatter landscape. Dirk could see the lightly coloured sand dunes from the front passenger seat. They were near to the coast.
In the road ahead, they could see a checkpoint and a barrier.
"Checkpoint. Is it normally heavily manned?" said Dirk.
"No," said van Kerk, adjusting his beret, and putting his foot down.
"Get ready men, we are near a checkpoint!"
Dirk leaned through the back of the windowless cabin and tapped his gun twice on the side of trailer. Two taps came back. "Get ready men," came a muffled response from the back of the trailer.
As the truck got nearer to the checkpoint, the wooden barrier started to slowly drop downwards, and van Kerk slowed down the truck, until it came to a stop amidst the squeaking noise of the brakes.
"Papers?" said the German soldier to van Kerk.
van Kerk handed over his real papers, and Dirk's forged papers.
"Farming at four a.m.?, a little early."
van Kerk shrugged, "I'm a busy farmer."
The German nodded and as the truck began to move forward they could hear a telephone ringing at the check

Five Days in May

point. Five seconds later three or four German guards were running around the checkpoint and shouting instructions to the other guards.
"Stop!" shouted the officer holding his hand up.
Van Kerk put his foot down and heard gun shots pinging off the cabin of the truck. Dirk and van Kerk flinched and sank down into their seats.
The deep sound of a Bren guns opened fire from the back of the truck "rat-tat-tat-tat". The checkpoint was peppered with bullets.
A couple of minutes later they were being pursued by the BMW motorbike with a side car (without its lights on) which had now easily caught up with the old overloaded truck. They drew level with the truck on the narrow road.
Major Carling climbed to the side of the trailer, pushed up the tarpaulin with one hand and rested his pistol against the side of the truck, took aim and shot the motorcyclist in his shoulder causing the bike to swerve off the road into the murky darkness. Carling noticed that the side car passenger appeared to be throwing something towards the truck before falling backwards out of the side car.
"Grenade!" shouted Major Carling, as he ripped the tarpaulin sheet away.
At the same time, Dirk saw two stick grenades roll off the Tarpaulin sheet into the back of the trailer.
"Grenade!!" shouted Bentley as mass panic broke out in the truck.
Bentley found the first grenade which rolled off the tarpaulin and into his onto his lap. He immediately threw it off the back of the truck. *There was one grenade left!.* Somebody fumbled around on the floor, whilst others began to leap off from the back of the truck.
"Jump!" shouted Dirk, as he opened the passenger door and leapt out of the cabin at the same time as van Kerk lost control of the steering wheel. The speeding truck ploughed through a low stone wall at the side of the road and tipped over sideways and slid across the field until it

Gary S Smith

came to crashing halt at a sand dune. The remaining men were thrown off the truck and landed in the sand. They scrambled on their hands and knees to distance themselves from the impending grenade explosion.

Five Days in May

Gary S Smith

CHAPTER TWENTY FOUR

THE NEW DAWN

Dawn, 30th September 1944.

The first grenade explosion killed Private Roberts who directly who took the full force of the blast. His tall figure lay spread eagled on the grass. There was a pause of a few seconds whilst the men ran and dived for cover and then the entire truck exploded. The large explosion of the truck was fueled by the ammunition stored in the truck. The flames sprung high into the night sky, and burning shrapnel shot off and fizzed into random directions.
"Stay down!" shouted Major Carling, but the scattered men were already pinned to the floor covering their heads waiting for the deadly fireworks to stop. The debris rained down hard, and it was clear to everyone that the Germans would now know their exact location.

Bentley looked round and saw a loose arm lying on the field next to him. One of the men, Jaap the giant Dutchman had been transformed into a human torch, arms flailing, screaming wildly. The other men tried to douse the flames with their jackets. It was hopeless. Van Kerk aimed his pistol at Jaap's charred, screaming body, and fired. The sound was almost drowned by the noise of the burning truck.

Major Carling limped over towards van Kerk where the survivors grouped together. He put a hand on van Kerk's shoulder.

Five Days in May

"How far to the boat?" said Carling.
"One Kilometer," said van Kerk spitting the sand from his mouth.
"I'm going to slow you down," said Major Carling holding his blood stained bandaged leg.
"Dirk and Downs take the Major to the boat; the others will cover your backs."
The 'others' consisted of van Kerk, Bentley, and Davis. They loaded up their weapons and pilfered whatever ammunition they could find around the truck and set off after the other three. Davis had a deep cut on his left arm, so Bentley tore off part of his shirt and tied around Davis's arm tightly.
"This way," said van Kerk as he started to jog towards the sand dunes.
 "We must get to the boat before daylight," said van Kerk.
As they moved across the sand dunes, they could see torch lights flickering in the distance moving towards the burning truck like moths to a flame. They looked for vantage point on top of a sand dune. Davis and Bentley set up the Bren guns and waited. "Me and Bentley will cover," said Davis in his thick Lancastrian accent.
Three shady figures were barely visible in the distance ahead. Carling limped on but in reality was half carried by Dirk and Downs.
As soon as the silhouettes of several German soldiers came over the sand dune and into the basin below them, Bentley threw two grenades over and Davis open fire with his Bren. Four Germans fell down. No more came.
Davis and Bentley picked up the Bren and hurried off to try and catch up with the others. The sand dunes seemed to provide some unwelcome brightness and visibility, and they could hear more German voices getting nearer.
Looking ahead Dirk could see the beach and a torch flashing up and down, making a V sign for the rendezvous.
"How far now?" said Bentley.
The six men raced across the soft sand, into the open flat

sands on the beach. They heard machine gun fire and bullets flying overhead.

Carling had his arms around the shoulders of Dirk and Downs. They took long strides, but the pace remained cumbersome. They were a big target for the Germans, who were following Carlings group.

More gunfire from the sand dunes they had just left. Carling was hit by a bullet that grazed the top of his shoulder, but he just grunted, and said nothing. He was already a liability to the others.

Downs felt the wind in his face as he turned towards the ocean, and he knew that Carling needed some cover. He stopped running.

"Dirk, you take the Major to the boat, I'll catch up with you," said Downs as he crouched to load his Sten gun.

Dirk didn't argue and continued to push the Major across the sands. They were both too tired to argue with Downs.

Downs scanned the sand dunes and he could see the silhouettes of at least seven or eight German soldiers standing at the bottom near the flat sands, firing their Schmeissers towards them. Van Kerk and other paras instantly took cover and lay down. When the firing stopped they could hear the sound of the waves on the beach. *Not far now.*

The others continued as Davis and Bentley also set up the Bren gun on the flat sand. Davis looked around at the flat expanse of the beach. It was only half dark now as dawn was approaching. They could see Downs parallel to them about 300 metres further down the beach blasting away with his Bren gun towards a separate group of cautiously approaching Germans.

Davis pulled the trigger and the bullets from the Bren scattered across the sand dunes. The Germans could not be seen anymore. It was time to run.

"We can't stay here. Nearly out of ammunition. No cover. they'll be more of them soon, let's go," said Bentley with

desperation in his voice, as he grabbed Davis by the shoulder.
Davis and Bentley ran towards the sea trying to catch up to the others. They looked around and saw Downs around twenty metres to their right now, lying down on his stomach spraying Bren gun bullets all over the sand dunes. He was the last man. Luckily they were all spread out across the beach.
As the Germans returned fire, Downs lay flat against the wet sand, his nose rubbing in the muddy sand. He could smell the salty sea water. The bullets landed around him, and with a deafening high pitched screech a bullet went through the side of his helmet and cut his ear. He felt the warm trickle of blood running down his neck. Firstly, he reached into his bag and awkwardly threw a smoke bomb across the sand. Maybe twenty metres away. As the smoke seeped out into the gloomy dawn he stood up tall the threw a grenade, maybe forty yards, then another, this time fifty yards. The grenades gained further distance by rolling on the flat sands towards the German soldiers.
Five seconds later two grenade explosions momentarily created chaos amongst the pursuers. Downs turned and sprinted towards the boat, his boots slapping hard against the wet sand. This was his chance to sprint away. Spurred on with grim reality of the becoming the last man in the fleeing pack.
"Come on Downs!" shouted Bentley.
Downs continued to sprint and turned to see that the smoke had been blown thin by the coastal breeze towards the sand dunes, the curtain was evaporating all too quickly. Now the cover had gone, and he instantly regretted staying behind to act as a decoy. Downs flinched as he heard the cracking noise of rifle shots. Bentley looked round and saw Downs stagger across the sand, clutching his stomach. He fell to his knees staring at his comrades as they continued to run. All he could see was multiple pairs of boots splashing across the shallow water towards the boat. They

all looked the same from a distance.

Suddenly there was a burst of Sten gun giving covering fire from the boat. The tracers flew over their heads towards the sand dunes. This was met with even more fire from the beach, who now seemed to have identified the location of the boat. A German mortar bomb landed in the wet sand causing a violent spray of mud, stinging the eyes of the men.
Now it was Davis's turn to run with the unwanted curse of being the last man. He had no ammunition, so he dropped his Sten gun. All he had left was a pistol with maybe three or four bullets left. He sprinted hard, panting heavily, tasting blood at the back of his throat, driven by the fear. The bullets whizzed past Davis, getting closer; Davis began to zig zag his run. A bullet struck the top of Downs's head, and a red jet of blood shot out diagonally into the air, and he collapsed to the ground in a staggering halt. He was already dead before his face fell onto the wet sand. The first shallow wave of sea water rippled over his forehead. The Lancashire grit would be washed away by the North Sea.

The four remaining men waded out to sea, unaware of their lost comrades, consumed with the urge to escape.
It was a small fishing boat and the old engine spurted out the diesel fumes. The man on the boat, was pointing his rifle at the Germans on the beach.
"Give us cover!" shouted the Major.
The men's arms moved quickly but legs were slowed down by the icy four foot waves crashing into them.
McKenzie was lying on the top of the captain's cabin firing his Bren gun across the sands. There had never been a better sight for the paras wading closer to the boat.
The Captain pulled up van Kerk first, then Dirk, and they began to drag the rest of the tired men into the boat, as the bullet splashed and fizzed through the water. Another

mortar landed in the sea, sending a jet of water high into the dawn sky. The boat rocked from side to side as Carling hoisted himself up with his arms with Bentley pushing him from behind.

Bentley's hands were clinging on to the side of the boat. The boat began to bob forwards over the choppy waves, slowly out to sea. Van Kerk the big Dutchman dragged Bentley onto the boat in one swift pull. At that moment Bentley's right calf took a bullet clean through it.
"Everyone lie flat," said Major Carling. The danger has not gone away.
The men took cover and lay flat at the bottom of the boat as the last bullets pinged against the sides. Each man was silent in his own prayer.
The icy winds of the ocean swept over them as they bounced forwards across the waves. McKenzie continued to spray the beach with bullets, but surprisingly the Germans remained distant, and they seemed to stop only half way across the beach.
The boat inched further and further away from the murderous beach into the unknown hostility of the cruel sea. It was the lesser of two evils. Gradually, they began to raise their heads when the bullets had stopped. The men shuffled around on the tightly packed old fishing boat, patching up their wounds. Bentley bandaged up Carling's leg wound once they had got the worst waves out of the way, and then vice versa. McKenzie pulled out a small piece of shrapnel sticking out from Dirk's foot.

Gradually, they left the port area and entered the open sea. The dawn was breaking to the east, as they headed north west towards England. The crew started to settle and embrace the prospect of surviving the last part of their mission. "McKenzie, you were a bit late to the party?" said Bentley.
"Aye. Luckily for me I landed on top of somebody's barn.

That *somebody* who knew van Kerk and Jaap. They also topped up my hip flask....I *really like* the Dutch people."

"Van Kerk. Why didn't the Germans follow us across the beach all the way to the boat?" said Carling.
"Because the beach is land-mined," said van Kerk, smiling grimly.
"...what?" said Bentley.
"It's okay, I knew a safe route, and marked it out with sticks last night," said Van Kerk
Dirk passed the packet of *Players* cigarettes around.
"I didn't see any sticks on the beach," said Dirk with a dry smile.
"...hhm...they got washed away by the tide...so I just guessed the route," said van Kerk.
Major Carling took a long drag on his cigarette.
There was some subdued laughter. The relief of survival.
"You Dutch guys are *crazy* bastards," said McKenzie.
The men became quiet and avoided eye contact. They looked out to sea, pretending to focus on the waves, but each man was deep within their own thoughts.

Dirk had always wanted the life of the soldier. That was up until now. The image of people like Jaap, Downs and Davis falling to their death's left indelible footprints in his mind that in later years, could never be erased. Not even the liquor can numb the mind completely of haunted memories. He had lost many friends in the cruel lottery of war, including Smit. Dirk tried to block out the ghost from the past by concentrating on his next visit to Christina in Tilburg.

"Bloody pity, the others couldn't make the boat trip," said Carling.
The others grunted in agreement. Nothing more could be said. Nobody spoke for a while, a respectful silence. The first tranche of survivor's guilt swept over them. There

Five Days in May

would be many more waves in a veteran's voyage into the post-war years of remembrance. McKenzie passed around his hip flask. This medicine was in demand.
The old trawler boat bobbed along the waves rocking the men from side to side. Bentley crawled under the tarpaulin of the fishing boat to go to sleep. He would sleep like a baby all the way to England. The loss of colleagues and friends like Davis and Downs, would be avenged with the death of more Nazis. Everybody had a different way of dealing with loss, there was no consistency in the grief of individuals.

Carling, Bentley, Dirk and McKenzie stayed outside, drinking and watching a new dawn. The adrenalin of their dramatic escape slowly oozed away, and tiredness had arrived just as the rest of the world was waking up to another day. To the east the rising winter sun was painting its murky canvas of orange, red, blue and grey clouds. Slowly, the splashes of orange became prominent.

Major Carling was making some scribbled notes in his pocket diary. He began writing the names of the soldiers and the Dutch resistance men who had distinguished themselves in the mission.
"Major Carling. Was the V-Rocket site destroyed? The mission was a success, right?" said Dirk.
Carling paused and smiled.
"Yes. We blew up (one of) the military bases which was firing the V-Rocket's, so we saved many civilians lives, maybe thousands. It was a tremendous show: against all odds," said Carling who removed his beret, instantly changing his appearance from commando leader to an ageing civilian now.
"But, I expect the enemy will have many more V-Rocket sites… so we just did our bit, British and Dutch alike," said Carling taking a drag on his pipe. Carling's authoritative answer seemed to underline a sense of

Gary S Smith

purpose for all the chaos, destruction and loss of life witnessed in the last two hours. Even McKenzie, a true cynic, was convinced.

Carling was an Oxford educated man, and a teacher before the war. He longed for the return of the academic life of the past. He loved reading, English literature classics such as Thomas Hardy, Dickens and Kipling. He stroked his mustache thoughtfully, half-drunk on bottled up fatigue and emotion. Although he adopted a paternal responsibility for his men he would never dream of sharing his true thoughts about war, with his men. That would be bad for morale, and inappropriate for a high ranking officer.
"We are like specks of dust in the winds of history," said Carling, muttering to himself, more like a philosopher than a Major. But the words were lost to the sound of the fresh ocean breeze. The men simply swayed gently from side to side following the rhythm of the waves, inching their way towards the safe shores of England.

****

Five Days in May

Gary S Smith

AUTHOR'S NOTE

This book tells the story of three Dutchmen: Kobus, Dirk and Smit. Although the names and character portrayals are fictional the inspiration for the story comes from family members involved in the war.

I was quite young when my Grandad died so I never really got to know him very well, but I was always proud that he'd flown a Spitfire during the war. I made a copy of his pilot log book, visited Kew (London archives) to obtain details of his missions. I was particularly interested in the conditions which the Photographic Reconnaissance Unit (PRU) pilots operated under. Single seater Spitfire, no guns, no radios; just a map, a camera and a parachute. The overall fatality rate of the Reconnaissance pilots was only 2%, which is surprisingly low considering that survival was based on being invisible and evading detection from enemy ground flak and fighter planes. The fatality rate was much higher for 'rookie' pilots, and also fighter pilots who joined the reconnaissance units and the latter apparently struggled to adapt to a different approach (i.e. evasion rather than engagement). The photographs obtained by the PRU were vital intelligence sources to the British intelligence for detecting the strengths and weaknesses of enemy forces, battleships, V-rocket launch pads, weapon factories and often formed the basis of allied military strategies. The importance of this aerial intelligence on air, land and sea operations is eloquently described in the *'Spies in the Sky'* book by Taylor Downing. Despite this critical contribution to the war effort, a depressing flip side (that I discovered at Kew Archives in London) was that the photographs of weapons factories handed to the RAF Bomber command resulted not only in bombing of factories but also with tragic collateral damage to Dutch towns and civilian casualties.

Johannes Van't Sant joined the army as an ordinary conscript in 1934, and was re-assigned to the 3rd Aviation Regiment in November 1938. His log book shows that he was present at three airfields in 1940 (Egmond, Waalhaven and Eindhoven). For the book I chose the location of Waalhaven airbase due to its size as it not only accommodated fighter planes, but also an army supply base, Koolhoven factory that manufactured the Fokker planes. The biggest airborne invasion in history (up until that point in time in May 1940) descended on a handful of strategic locations, including Waalhaven.

My Grandad's military record showed that he'd left the Netherlands on 15th May 1940, arrived in France on 18th May 1940 and arrived in England on 29th May 1940. He joined the RAF in 1941, qualified as a pilot and flew for six months (16 missions) in 1942/1943 across France, Belgium, Holland and Germany. Johannes's first mission In August 1942, was to fly from England to Rotterdam (his home town), take photographs, and return. I cannot imagine what he would have thought when he saw the destruction, and levelling of his former home city from 25,000 feet.

I have tried very hard to stay faithful to the historical facts in the book, especially the invasion of Rotterdam and the experiences of RAF reconnaissance missions. The fictional aspect is clearly the personalities of the characters and the human conditions involved in the theatre of war. Thousands of Dutch soldiers escaped from the Netherlands in 1940 and made their perilous journey across France, often being strafed by enemy aircraft.

My main inspiration for the book came from my Grandad's sister-in-law, Simon Van Kampen. Simon produced a family tree (when he was well into his eighties, In 2005) showing the history of the Van't Sants. I noticed that George Frans Van't Sant and George Frans Hooyer had both died at an early age during the Nazi occupation. I started to ask questions and although Simon did not have much detail about the two "George Frans's" who were killed, he gave me so much information about his own personal experiences (through numerous letters) during the war, that I began to understand the long and chaotic evacuation of hundreds of thousands of troops who travelled west across mainland Europe, the channel, and finally to Britain where lifelong relationships were formed.

Unfortunately, I never had chance to meet Simon as he passed away shortly after our exchange of letters but I am eternally thankful for his wonderfully written letters describing the emotional events of 1940 that changed so many lives. I will certainly treasure these letters.

The family tree compiled by Simon showed that two young men on the "Dutch side" of my family were involved in the Dutch resistance and were subsequently killed by the Nazis.

George Frans Van't Sant (my Grandad's brother) was an active member of the resistance helping people 'in hiding', ('*onderduikers*') until he was arrested and transported to Bergen-Belsen concentration camp where he died (approximate age of 25).

Then there was George Frans Hooyer (my Grandad's nephew). His resistance activities are not fully known, except that he escaped the Netherlands in in 1943 via France, Spain, Morroco (Algiers) to finally reach England to meet up with his uncle (Johannes Van't Sant) in London. Hooyer becomes involved with the British intelligence services and was parachuted into the East of Holland, conducted telegraphs several pieces of valuable information back to the British intelligence until in 1943 he was arrested in the Hague Shot by the Gestapo in Rotterdam 12th March 1945 (Age 21).

Whilst researching the book, I was surprised to discover how little I knew about the Nazi invasion Netherlands in May 1940. Furthermore, there are very few publications in English on this subject, with *"Winter in Wartime"* (by Jan Terouw) being an exceptional and rare novel that seems to capture the desperation (and the dilemmas) facing the Dutch people during the 1940-1945

Gary S Smith

occupation. Historians should consider the contrast between the British outlook on WWII compared to the outlook of the occupied nations in Europe. The British war experience is retrospectively packaged by the media (mostly driven by Hollywood) into only a few events such as Dunkirk, the 'Battle of Britain,' and D-Day. This book introduces a new perspective: a view from an occupied nation. I hope you enjoyed reading it and found it interesting.

Five Days in May

ABOUT THE AUTHOR

The author lives with his wife and family in Berkshire, England.

Gary S Smith

Printed in Great Britain
by Amazon